Bestall

This book belongs to

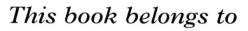

CONTENTS

Edited by Thomas McBrien. Designed by Pritty Ramjee.
Cover illustrated by Stuart Trotter.
Endpapers illustrated by Alfred Bestall.

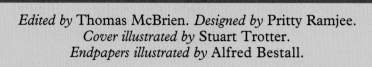

THE
RUPERT ®
ANNUAL

Rupert and the Time Machine is an original Egmont UK creation.
The author and illustrator, Stuart Trotter, has combined the duotone style
used in 1920 with the full-colour anthropomorphic style used today, to pay
homage to the Rupert Bear illustrations over the last hundred years.

EXPRESS NEWSPAPERS

EGMONT
We bring stories to life

First published in Great Britain in 2020 by Egmont Books UK Limited
2 Minster Court, 10th floor, London EC3R 7BB
Rupert Bear™ & © Express Newspapers & DreamWorks Distribution Limited.
All Rights Reserved.

ISBN 978 1 4052 9646 5
70843/001
Printed in Italy

Picture credits: cover, p4 pondkungz/shutterstock

No. 85

RUPERT'S

When Rupert answers his friend's distress signal a great underwater journey begins for the little bear. There are unexpected thrills, and dangers too, then he receives a gift more precious than any amount of gold the Professor might find.

RUPERT BEGINS HIS HOLIDAY

The little bear is on his way,
With Mummy, for a holiday.

A bus takes them the last few miles,
"How blue the sea is!" Rupert smiles.

It is holiday time and Mrs Bear has decided to take Rupert to Greyport, a seaside place. "We've never been there before, have we, Mummy?" says Rupert. "Is it as nice as Sandy Bay and Greyrocks Cove?" "Yes, I think so," replies Mrs Bear. "Daddy suggested we should go there for a change, and he has found us somewhere to stay." "Won't it be lovely to have two whole weeks by the sea?" murmurs Rupert. "I'm looking forward to it so much." When the excitement of packing is over Mr Bear sees them off by train and soon they have reached the big station at Nutchester. "Come on, we must change here," says Mrs Bear. "Our shortest way now is by bus." The new part of the country is full of interest to Rupert and, kneeling at the window, he watches all that passes until he gives a cry. "Look, there's the sea, Mummy! How blue it is!"

DEEP SEA ADVENTURE

RUPERT DASHES ON AHEAD

Oh, Mummy, Greyport's simply grand!
I only wish there was more sand."

A figure catches Rupert's eye,
He dashes forward, with a cry.

The bus continues along a pretty coast-road until they reach Greyport. "May I go down to the shore?" asks Rupert, as soon as they have arrived in the town. "It's rather late now," Mummy tells him. "We must find our way to the place where we are going to stay, then there are our bags to unpack. You'll have plenty of time to explore tomorrow." So Mrs Bear and Rupert settle into their rooms on the first evening, and the next day they climb to a point from which they can see the whole sweep of the bay and the busy little port below them. "There doesn't seem to be much sand to play in," says Rupert. "I expect there will be lots of other things to do. Shall we go down and explore the town?" They leave the high ground and make for the main street. Suddenly Mrs Bear is surprised to hear Rupert give a shout, and he darts ahead waving his arms wildly as he goes.

RUPERT GREETS THE DWARF

The dwarf turns, with a startled glance,
Then cries, "This is a lucky chance!"

"My master has a secret plan,
Meet us tomorrow, if you can!"

Next morning, Mummy wants to rest,
"So join your friends, that would be best."

The old Professor's smiling face
Greets Rupert at the meeting-place.

Running down almost to the quay Rupert catches up with a small figure whom he has spied. It is the old Professor's dwarf servant and Rupert greets him happily. "Fancy finding you in the very place we've come for our holiday! Are you staying here, too?" When Mrs Bear joins them the dwarf turns to her with some eagerness. "I think Rupert is just the person my master would like to see," he says. "May he join us tomorrow? Please don't ask me why. It's for a very secret reason!"

Before leaving his friends the dwarf suggests a place where Rupert may meet him and next morning Mrs Bear thinks it over. "I don't like it being so secret," says she. "But the Professor is a very kind old gentlemen and I should be able to trust you with him, so I'll cut you a bag of sandwiches, but be sure to come back for tea. Meanwhile I'll have a nice quiet day here." After breakfast Rupert sets off. Even so, the Professor and his servant are on the spot before him.

RUPERT'S WEIGHT IS NOTED

The old man says, "First we must stop,
And weigh you in this chemist's shop."

He makes a note of Rupert's weight,
Then smiles, "That's right, at any rate."

A few doors down, they stop again.
"Come in," he beams, "and I'll explain."

"This map I've found is very old,
It marks a wreck, with sunken gold!"

Hurrying to join his friends Rupert is very inquisitive to know why he has been sent for. At first the old gentleman only smiles mysteriously. "Let's start by going in here," he murmurs. "This is the only chemist's shop in the town." "Oh, what are you going to buy?" asks the little bear. "Nothing!" says the old gentleman, smiling more broadly. "Come over here." And leading Rupert across he stands him on the weighing machine and gazes intently at the dial. Then he gives a satisfied chuckle. Before Rupert can ask any more questions the Professor leaves the shop and takes him to another doorway. "This is a cottage I have taken for the summer," he says, and leads the little bear inside. "I think you will be interested in my little invention. But first let me tell you something else that will explain why my servant and I have come to this quiet out-of-the-way place." Then, turning to a shelf, he picks up a roll of brownish paper and spreads it on the table.

RUPERT IS MEASURED NEXT

The old man whispers, "Here's the spot!
Now, is that gold still there or not?"

His servant measures Rupert's height,
And tells his master, "That's just right."

"I've made two diving-suits in all,
My servant's, though, has come too small."

"Please try it on, it's just your size,
And test it, please," the old man cries.

"Now look," says the Professor. "This is an ancient map that I have discovered. It is of this coast and, see, it marks a wreck out in the bay. I believe that wreck still has some gold in it!" Then he gets up abruptly and puts the map away. "I say, how topping!" cries Rupert. "But why did you send for *me*? And what is your invention?" Instead of answering the Professor whispers to his servant, who starts carefully to measure Rupert's height. Still smiling, the Professor holds something he has taken from a box. "To get at the wreck one must dive," says the old man. "So I've invented a new diving-suit. I made another for my servant, but it turned out to be too small and I do believe it is just your size, so try it on." He lifts another garment from the box. In a few minutes Rupert is dressed in the suit, and then the dwarf helps him into a large headpiece made of hard plastic with two holes through which he is told to put his arms. "But how can I breathe in this?" asks Rupert.

RUPERT LIKES HIS NEW OUTFIT

He puts two pills in, with great care,
To fill the headpiece with fresh air.

"That shows you how the air's supplied
For deep-sea diving, if you tried."

"No, Rupert, you can't dive today.
Whatever would your Mummy say?"

They all set off along the pier,
A motor-boat is moored quite near.

Rupert's question is soon answered. Taking a couple of small pills from a tiny box the Professor puts them into a black box on the left side of the suit and turns a switch. Immediately Rupert's big headpiece is filled with air. "There, those are my greatest invention," says the old gentleman. "They are air pellets that would give you air to breathe for hours under water." "It feels lovely," Rupert laughs, and capers about. "Now may I go diving with you?" When the wonderful suit is removed Rupert is in great excitement. "Oh, please *may* I put it on again and go down under the sea?" he begs. "No, you certainly *may* not," chuckles the Professor. "Whatever would your mother say if I let you run risks like that! But I tell you what, the sea is calm today so you may watch me go down in search of that ancient wreck if you like." The dwarf servant packs both diving-suits carefully into a strong case and soon they are all walking through the sunshine towards the sea.

RUPERT HAS A BOAT-TRIP

"That heavy sack must weigh you down,"
Says Rupert, with a puzzled frown.

"Some weight, you'll see, is what we need!"
The servant smiles, and off they speed.

When Greyport's almost out of sight,
The old man says, "This spot seems right."

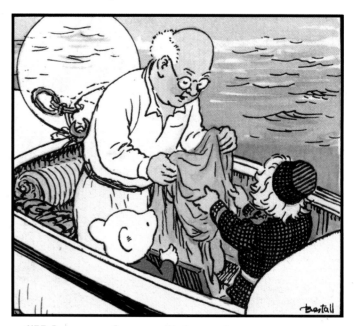

"Help me to don my diving-suit,
And screw the weight on to each boot!"

Near the end of the pier a flight of stone steps leads down nearly to the water, and there Rupert sees a smart motor-boat which the Professor enters. "That's a fearfully heavy sack you're carrying," says the little bear as he notices the dwarf servant struggling behind. "There's more in it than just the other headpiece," answers the dwarf. "You'll see in good time." He lowers it carefully into the boat. And without waiting they head out to sea. "How lucky it's so fine and calm," says the Professor. "It's just the sort of day I need for this job." When they are well out to sea the Professor stops the boat frequently, each time gazing back intently through field glasses towards different parts of the land now so far away. "My points are all in line," he mutters at length. "This should be the exact spot." While Rupert watches, he removes his blazer. The dwarf servant holds up the diving-suit that he has taken from the case and the old gentleman begins to put it on.

RUPERT BECOMES EXCITED

"Without these weights I'd only float,
And sink no lower than this boat."

The old man puts the air-pills in,
Now he is ready to begin.

Slowly he sinks beneath a wave,
While Rupert gasps and says, "How brave!"

"My master jerked the rope to show
He's reached the sea-bed, far below."

Rupert gazes fascinated at the preparations for diving. "Are you really going down now?" he breathes. "I'm not quite ready yet," smiles the Professor. "If I went down like this I shouldn't sink." He sits down while the dwarf lifts two very heavy objects from the sack, fits them over the Professor's boots, and screws them on. Then the old gentleman uses the pellets to fill his plastic headpiece with air, and lastly the dwarf threads the rope through the prow and secures it to the loop on the diving-suit. At length the Professor is satisfied that all is fixed correctly, and he slips cheerfully into the water. Rupert watches nervously and is a little scared as the old gentleman disappears. "How brave he is!" he quavers. The dwarf is intent on the machinery that lets out the rope gently. More and more is unwound until he reaches out and stops it. "There was a jerk on the rope," he exclaims. "That's my master's signal to show he's on the bottom of the sea!"

RUPERT SENSES DANGER

Smiles Rupert Bear, "I'll have my snack,
Until it's time to pull him back."

The strong rope gives a double jerk,
"Quick, little bear, let's get to work!"

The rope will only wind so far,
And then it stops, with such a jar.

Alas, the servant tries in vain
To pull his master up again.

Now the two friends have to wait for a long time. The dwarf keeps a slight strain on the rope in case a message comes from the old Professor who is walking about the sea-bed, and Rupert takes his chance to eat his sandwiches while a sharp-eyed seagull flies around hopefully. All at once the dwarf stiffens and becomes more alert. "There was a tug on the rope," he mutters. "Yes, and there's another! That means my master wants to be pulled up again. Quick, we must now get to work at once."

Scrambling down from his perch Rupert watches the dwarf pushing a couple of knobs and pulling a lever. At once the top cylinder begins to turn, winding the rope slowly and steadily. Suddenly it stops with a jerk. The dwarf works the lever, but nothing happens. "The rope's caught on something!" he cries. He goes forward and drags on it with all his might. "My poor master's in trouble somewhere down below. Unless he can manage to free the rope he's stuck – and so are we!"

Across the vessel Rupert crawls,
"There's nothing to be seen," he calls.

"I'll have to dive and free the rope!
Please let me, it's our only hope!"

"All right then, as we have no choice,"
The dwarf says, in a shaky voice.

The second rope is soon prepared,
"That's fine," nods Rupert, "don't be scared!"

Rupert peers into the deep water. "There's nothing to be seen at all down there," he says, and he crawls rapidly back to his friend. "That other diving-suit," he cries. "It's much too small for you but *it fits me*! Why shouldn't I put it on and go down and try to free that rope?" The dwarf looks aghast. "No, no, the Professor would never allow that," he says huskily. "It's far too risky." "Well, but what other way can you think of to get us out of this terrible fix?" asks Rupert urgently. Seeing there is no choice the dwarf picks the other diving-suit out of the case and, looking very worried indeed, helps Rupert into it. Next he screws the heavy weights to his feet and turns the switch so that the plastic headpiece fills with air. "The Professor provided two cylinders of rope," he says, "so that he and I could take turns to go down if that suit had fitted me." He threads the second rope through the prow and then ties it firmly to the loop on Rupert's diving-suit.

RUPERT DESCENDS IN SEARCH

The sea below looks very deep,
As Rupert Bear prepares to leap.

Down, down, through dim green depths he sinks,
"It's like a new world," Rupert thinks.

Far down, he spies some jagged beams,
He's reached that ancient wreck, it seems.

He lands upon the ocean bed,
And finds his old friend, just ahead.

When all is ready Rupert drags his heavy feet to the prow and the dwarf, looking as anxious as ever, prepares to control the second cylinder. "When the Professor went in he seemed to think it was quite a joke," says the little bear, nervously, "so it can't be too bad. I wonder if it will be very cold." Screwing up his courage he jumps from the boat with a slight splash. In a moment he is dropping slowly and steadily through a new world, dim, greenish, and very silent – down, down, down! Rupert's descent is so steady and quiet, and the fishes he can see are so interesting, that he soon forgets to feel frightened. To his relief the diving-suit keeps him quite warm and he finds that he can breathe easily. When he is a long way down some jagged shapes appear. "Those must be the remains of the wreck that the Professor wanted," he murmurs. At length he reaches the ocean bed and turns round slowly. "Why, surely there is the Professor himself!" he gasps in surprise.

RUPERT FREES THE PROFESSOR

Pleads Rupert, "Don't be cross with me!
I had to dive, to set you free."

"The rope has got caught up somehow,
So I'll climb up and free it now."

"It's caught around this point of wood!
I've pulled it free!" he gasps. "Oh, good!"

His friend comes up with such a lurch
That Rupert's bumped right off his perch!

Now that he is so far under the water Rupert finds to his delight that he can walk quite easily in spite of the weights on his feet, and in a moment he is facing the astonished old gentleman. "Rupert!" gasps the Professor. "Didn't I tell you not to . . ." "Oo, how topping," Rupert interrupts. "We can hear each other quite clearly, even through these head things! The dwarf said you were stuck so I came down. Now I'll free you." And he starts to climb to the rotting timbers. Rupert scrambles well above the Professor and, sure enough, he discovers that the rope has caught around a curved point of wood. Leaning back he pulls with all his might and just manages to free it. The rope straightens and the old gentleman comes up so suddenly that he bumps Rupert off his perch. Before the Professor disappears on his way to the surface the little bear hears him call out: "Don't worry. We'll pull you up to safety as soon as I have reached the boat."

RUPERT DRIFTS DOWNWARD

He feels a tug, then starts to rise.
"They're pulling me up now!" he cries.

"The wreck!" cries Rupert Bear, aghast,
"It's caught me up, I can't get past!"

He dangles there, all movement stops,
Then, just as suddenly, he drops!

"The wreck has frayed my rope right through!"
Groans Rupert. "Now what shall I do?"

Still feeling very light Rupert falls slowly until he settles gently back on the ocean bed where he is surrounded by inquisitive fishes. He stands up and waits, then there is a tug on the rope and he is being pulled upwards. Almost at once the rising stops and he hangs helplessly with his back pressing against something hard. "Oh dear, what a noodle I am," he cries. "Why didn't I move away from the wreck? Now I'm stuck just as the Professor was!" For a few minutes Rupert remains fixed. Then, just as suddenly, the pressure on his back ceases and he drifts easily downwards. "My, the Professor's been quick if he's returned and set me free already!" he thinks. But when he is on the seabed there is no sign of the old gentleman and he gazes around puzzled. "W-where is he?" wonders the little bear. Gradually an awful thought strikes him, and he feels the loop at his back. "The rope isn't there!" he gasps. "It's broken! I must have been jammed against a sharp edge of iron!"

RUPERT SWEEPS FARTHER ON

"The old Professor will find out,
He'll come for me, without a doubt."

Just then, a current knocks him back,
It swirls him onwards in its track.

Though Rupert grasps some seaweed strands,
They only slip straight through his hands.

He's swept towards a rocky space,
And drifts into a calmer place.

At first Rupert is horrified, realising that there is now nothing connecting him to the boat. Then he calms down. "The Professor is sure to come back for me," he thinks. "I'd better move away from the wreck." He tries to reach a limpet-covered rock not far away. "This is queer," he mutters. "I can hardly keep my feet over here." And when he tries to sit down he cannot do so, for he has entered a current which swirls him right away. Rupert tries desperately to check his head-long journey as the current drives him faster and faster through masses of seaweed. He grabs at some of the long strands, but they are too smooth and slip through his hands. At length he is caught by a side eddy and drifts through a gap in some rocks into quiet water. "This is dreadful, I'm trapped at the bottom of the sea!" he moans when he has gained his feet. "The Professor could never find me now! I can't possibly find my way back against that strong current."

RUPERT IS NO LONGER ALONE

"My friends will never find me here,"
Thinks Rupert, quivering with fear.

"Without these weights I'd surely rise,
But I can't get them off," he sighs.

The Merboy swims up for a chat,
He laughs, "Oh, what a funny hat!"

"You'll guide me home, you never fail!"
Delighted, Rupert tells his tale.

Walking carefully so as not to be caught in the current again, Rupert finds himself at the foot of a cliff. More strange fish come and stare, but do not touch him. All at once an idea comes to him. "If only I could get these great irons off my boots I should float straight up to the surface," he thinks. But, alas, he cannot do it. His huge gauntlets can hardly reach his boots, and while he is struggling he does not notice who is approaching from above. At the sound of a silvery laugh, Rupert stands up suddenly. "Is it the Merboy?" he gasps. "Surely it can't be!" "Well, well," chuckles the little creature. "The fishes said there was someone here. Fancy it being *you*! What are you doing at the bottom of the sea? And in that funny hat?" "Oo, how glad I am to see you!" cries Rupert. "I never expected to find a friend down here." Quickly he tells the whole story and asks the Merboy to show him how he can get back to the boat and the Professor. "Only you can help me," he says.

20

RUPERT DARE NOT LET GO

"First," smiles the Merboy, "come and meet
King Neptune – as his birthday treat!"

"We'll show him what a diver's like,"
He says. "Just hold on to that spike!"

That jagged object Rupert grasps,
Then, "Hi, it's moving up!" he gasps.

"Hang on!" he hears the Merboy say.
"Our wise sea-serpent knows the way!"

The Merboy gets very excited. "I'll help you, of course," he says, "but I've just had such a jolly idea. Today is King Neptune's birthday. I'll show you to him. He has never seen anything like you. It will be a great treat for him! Then you can go home." Taking Rupert's hand, he swims strongly until he reaches what looks like a long rock covered with large spikes. "Hold very tight to one of those spikes," says the Merboy, "and don't be surprised at anything that happens while I'm away." Rupert obediently holds tight to one of the rocky spikes while the Merboy swims rapidly forward and disappears. "Where has he gone? And why am I to stick on here?" Rupert muses. He soon finds the answer. "Hi, this isn't a rock. It's beginning to rise!" he gasps. And, sure enough, while he clings on he is carried up through the water until suddenly he is out in the sunlight. Ahead of him his little friend is moving back towards him. "How d'you like our sea-serpent?" smiles the Merboy.

RUPERT LOSES THE MERBOY

The water round them swirls and seethes,
"It's like a switchback!" Rupert breathes.

The serpent's pace becomes quite slow,
And now the Merboy dives below.

That creature sinks, then all alone,
On to the sea-bed Rupert's thrown.

Says Rupert, "What a funny thing,
I think that it is beckoning!"

Rupert takes some time to get used to the surprise of being carried by a sea-serpent, and he has to cling on more firmly than ever as the great creature puts on speed until it is tearing through the surface of the waves. Gradually some small, jagged islands appear. As the sea-serpent approaches them it begins to slow down and starts to sink. Then, without a word, the Merboy dives from it and disappears. "Oh, please don't leave me now!" Rupert cries. "Must I stay here on the sea-serpent?" The creature sinks steadily and slowly until it is near the floor of the ocean. Then without warning it gives a mighty shrug and a wiggle and Rupert is shaken off into a bed of seaweed. He struggles to his feet and, perching on a rock, he looks round. The Merboy is nowhere to be seen, but on a nearby boulder another creature is gazing at him and waving a tentacle. "I do believe it is beckoning to me," he murmurs. "Perhaps I'd better follow it and see."

RUPERT FACES KING NETPUNE

Beside a tunnel Rupert sees
A fish, who calls, "Step right in, please!"

The Merboy parts a seaweed screen,
Then Rupert sees a dazzling scene.

Upon a throne where coral gleams,
Old Father Neptune sits and beams.

King Neptune cries, "I do declare!
A visitor – a little bear!"

The strange creature leads Rupert round an angle of the rock and squats beside the entrance to a low tunnel. Immediately there appear four sea horses and a gorgeous fish and a black crab. "Hurry up," says the fish. "They're waiting for you." "What!" cries Rupert. "Were you expecting me?" Timidly he passes through the tunnel and there before him is the Merboy smiling and holding aside a seaweed curtain through which the little bear can see a brightly lit cave. "Come on. In you go!" says the Merboy. When the seaweed curtain closes behind him Rupert is suddenly face to face with an extraordinary figure holding a trident and seated on a coral throne. "It's Father Neptune, our King," whispers the little Merboy. The old gentleman rises and walks round and round Rupert, touches the plastic headpiece and gazes in wonder at him. "Well, well, well," he laughs in delight. "A real little bear at the bottom of the sea! You've come on my birthday, too."

RUPERT ADMIRES THE SHELLS

King Neptune lifts his hands in glee,
Then laughs, "How came you here to me?"

Asks Rupert, when his tale is told,
"Please, does that old wreck carry gold?"

"No gold is worth the risks you took!
My shells are worth far more – just look!"

Each shell with wondrous colour glows,
Says Neptune, "Gold could not buy those!"

King Neptune continues to laugh with glee at the sight of Rupert. "That Merboy has certainly given me a lovely birthday surprise," he chuckles, "but tell me, how came a little bear here?" "It's like this," replies Rupert. "My clever friend, the old Professor, invented these diving-suits to explore that ancient wreck near Greyport to see if there was gold in it. My rope broke and I was swept away. Oh, please, you know everything down here. Do tell me. *Is* there any gold in that wreck?"

King Neptune makes a strange answer to Rupert's question. "*Gold*?" he cries. "Your old Professor was not at all clever to risk his life and yours for anything so silly as gold!" He gives an order and another weird creature lifts a large shell. In it are smaller shells of the most unearthly, glowing colours. "Ooooh, how lo-o-ovely!" gasps Rupert. "Now, little bear," says King Neptune. "Tell your friend the Professor that all the gold in the world could not make the beauty of one of those!"

RUPERT MUST MAKE HASTE

Then Neptune, with a happy smile,
Speaks with the Merboy for a while.

"The King himself will take you home,
Right royally, across the foam!"

From Rupert comes a worried shout,
"My air supply is giving out!"

"Quick," cries the Merboy, "you must climb
These rocky steps! You'll just have time."

For some time Rupert looks in wonder at the marvellous shells. When he turns round he notices that the Merboy and King Neptune are deep in conversation. Then the Merboy swims towards him. "Father Neptune is so pleased to have seen you that he says he will take you home himself," he smiles. "That is a very, very great honour. When would you like to start?" "Please, I ought to go at once," says Rupert. "My Mummy will be getting anxious about me, and so, I expect, will the Professor!" The Merboy goes to tell King Neptune of Rupert's decision and when he returns he finds the little bear very worried. "Something's gone wrong," says Rupert. "I'm finding it hard to breathe. The Professor's air pellets must be giving out! What can I do?" "No time to lose! Quick, follow me," cries the Merboy. He darts sideways round a rock and Rupert sees a flight of rough steps. As fast as he can he stumbles up them, his feet getting heavier and heavier as he climbs.

RUPERT CAN BREATHE FREELY

"Help me to get this suit undone!"
Gasps Rupert, blinking in the sun.

His little friend works very fast.
And Rupert breathes fresh air at last.

He soon recovers from his shock,
Then drags the suit on to a rock.

The Merboy smiles, "Now you're all right!"
He dives, and vanishes from sight.

Just as he feels he can climb no further Rupert realises that his head is out of the water. Filled with new hope, he struggles still higher, dragging his heavy, weary feet on to the final step until he is at last on a dry rock. In his clumsy gloves he cannot set himself free, but he tells the Merboy what to do. His little friend quickly opens the diving-suit and at last Rupert is taking deep breaths of sweet, fresh air. "Whew! You got me out of that in the nick of time!" he gasps. For some minutes Rupert rests after his struggle up the underwater steps and enjoys being out of the strange headpiece. Then he seizes the diving-suit with its heavy irons on the feet and drags it clear of the sea. "We must save that at all costs," he mutters. "It belongs to the Professor." "Good, you're all right now," says the Merboy cheerfully. "I must go." And he dives away from the rock. "Oh dear," cries Rupert. "I do wish he wouldn't keep leaving me like this! I don't like being left alone so often."

RUPERT GETS A GREAT SHOCK

A flock of seabirds gather round,
They scatter, at a splashing sound.

White horses, in a cloud of spray,
Have frightened all those birds away!

The laughing Merboy reappears,
Just as a new sea-serpent nears.

Then Rupert, with a startled cry,
Is firmly gripped, and swung on high!

Soon after the Merboy has vanished into the ocean a flock of birds appears from nowhere, hovering and perching and staring at Rupert curiously. "They've never seen a bear before," he thinks. Then something disturbs them and they wheel away sharply just as a burst of foam breaks the quiet surface of the sea. Rupert gets up and gazes at the great cloud of spray. "What is it now?" he quavers. "I do believe I can see white horses there! And behind them surely – yes, it is! It's King Neptune himself!" Rupert watches, fascinated, while the whirling cloud of spray passes and disappears round the island. As soon as the sea has calmed down a familiar figure bobs up just below him. "Now then, we shan't be long," the Merboy smiles. "Look who's coming." "Not *another* sea-serpent!" gasps Rupert. "It's a different shape. What have I to do now?" "Just lie down and wait," laughs the Merboy. Next moment Rupert is seized by his jersey and lifted away.

27

RUPERT RIDES IN FINE STYLE

Next, Rupert spies a glinting crown,
And feels himself swung gently down.

Before him, smiling Neptune stands,
With reins and trident in his hands.

Cries Rupert, leaning from the shell,
"Here comes my diving-suit as well!"

Now Rupert has a thrilling ride,
As through the waves they swiftly glide.

When Rupert has recovered his wits he sees the wavelets passing beneath him and the sea-serpent swings him away from the island and dumps him into something hard and firm. Picking himself up Rupert sees that he is in a huge shell and the figure of Father Neptune is before him. "Well, little bear," says the tall monarch heartily. "Have you no word for me? Nay, do not look worried. My Merboy has everything under control. Your precious diving-suit will follow. You just trust yourself to me." Peering around the strange new ship Rupert sees in front the two white horses he had spied from the island, curvetting and splashing impatiently. In good time the sea-serpent returns, bearing the diving-suit which he drops on board, and without a moment's delay King Neptune gives a cry, the horses rear and plunge, and away they go faster and faster, the great shell skimming the waves like a chariot. Rupert is thrilled. "This is the loveliest journey I've ever had," he breathes.

RUPERT SITS ON A TURTLE

"Your homeland lies just over there,
I can't go nearer, little bear."

"Here's something from my treasure chest,
To show you've been my birthday guest!"

"My turtles' backs are strong and broad!"
Then Rupert Bear is placed aboard.

"This turtle makes a splendid ship,
But I must take care not to slip."

Rupert is nearly breathless from the great speed at which the big shell has travelled. Again without warning Father Neptune checks the white horses and they stop in another burst of spray. "There's your land, little bear," he says. "Nearer I must not go. There may be ships and I must not be seen by men. Here is a parting gift for you. Open it when you get home." And he hands over a small package. "Oo, thank you!" cries Rupert. "But, please, if you are dropping me here how *do* I travel the rest of the way home?" In answer to this question Rupert is told to look over the side, and there, close beside the great shell, he sees two large, brownish, floating objects. "My ocean-going turtles will finish the journey for you," declares King Neptune. The little bear is lifted on to one of the turtles, while the other carries the diving-suit and tows the floating headpiece. Then with a cry of farewell the king leaves him. "Oh dear, this is a wobbly perch!" mutters Rupert. "I hope I shan't slip off!"

RUPERT ARRIVES AT LONG LAST

The Merboy bobs up with a smile,
And laughs, "I've been here all the while!"

"Goodbye! I must return," he cries,
"I daren't be seen by human eyes."

The Boy Scout, Geoffrey, turns and stares,
"I must be dreaming!" he declares.

Then Rupert gives a joyful shout,
And waves to the astonished Scout.

Before Rupert has gone far with the turtles, he is aware that someone is swimming beside him. "Why, it's the Merboy!" he cries. "Where *have* you come from? We left you behind at the jagged islands." "Oh no, you didn't," laughs the Merboy, "I've been ahead of you all the time. And I arranged for these turtles to act as your landing craft! I'd lead you ashore, but I can see a human being there, so I must go. Goodbye, Rupert!" And he dives quickly into the sea and disappears.

Geoffrey, the Boy Scout, has been searching for rare shells on the shore. A cloud of spray far out at sea has attracted his attention and as he stares it fades and vanishes, leaving some small dark objects that float slowly over the calm sea straight towards him. Speechless with astonishment, he watches two turtles and a little bear struggling up the shingle. "My, I'm glad there's somebody here!" cries Rupert. "Please, where are we? D'you know these parts well? Are we anywhere near Greyport?"

RUPERT DRAGS THE HEAVY SUIT

"Please help me bring my suit up here,
Before those turtles disappear!"

Says Rupert, with an anxious frown,
"We cannot drag this right to town."

"We'll leave it, and fetch someone strong,
To help us bring the suit along."

Across the rock-strewn shore they tread,
Towards Greyport, not far ahead.

At length the Scout Geoffrey pulls himself together and answers Rupert's questions. "Yes, Greyport is just around the corner of the cliff," he says. "But surely you're the missing bear! Everybody's talking about you. Wherever have you been all this time?" "Please don't ask me just now," Rupert smiles. "I want help to drag that heavy diving-suit up the beach to safety." Geoffrey hurries to lend a hand. Then, relieved of their loads, the two great turtles swim away and disappear far out to sea. The diving-suit has such heavy boots that Rupert and the Scout soon tire of pulling it along. "I have an idea," says Geoffrey. "Let's drag it well above high-tide mark and remember the spot. Then somebody stronger can help us fetch it later on." So they find a safe place for it. "Now come on," says Geoffrey. "Your friends must see you at once, but you must promise to tell me the whole story soon." They clamber along the rocks until at last Greyport appears.

RUPERT ASTOUNDS EVERYONE

That fisherman swings round and starts,
As up the pier steps Rupert darts!

He spreads his happy news around,
"The little bear is safe and sound!"

"Rupert's returned! It's past belief!"
The people say, in great relief.

The old Professor holds him high,
And greets him with a joyful cry.

As the two friends near the end of their journey a fisherman spies them and stares as if he cannot believe his eyes when they climb the steps at the side of the stone pier. Then, without a word, he turns and runs into the village. "What's the matter with that man?" Rupert asks. "You've given him a shock," Geoffrey smiles. "Nobody here expected to see you again. Let's hurry if you're not too tired. There should be some fun when we reach your people." "I'll be glad to see them!" cries Rupert.

Round the next corner Rupert sees that the fisherman has joined a group and in the middle of them is the Professor. "Rupert!" he gasps. "But what . . . but how . . ." Almost speechless he lifts the little bear and gazes closely at him. "Yes, yes, you're real!" he breathes. "Of course I am," laughs Rupert. "I always have been!" Meanwhile the dwarf, equally amazed, turns to Geoffrey. "You brought him," he says. "How did he get back here? Have you any idea?"

RUPERT HUGS HIS MUMMY

Upon his shoulder Rupert's perched.
"Where did you go? We searched and searched."

"Oh, Rupert! Is that really you?"
Gasps Mummy. "Quickly, say it's true!"

With hugs, the great adventure ends.
Cries Rupert, "Please don't blame my friends!"

He shows King Neptune's gift, with pride.
"For you!" he laughs. "Let's go inside!"

Geoffrey tries to answer the dwarf. "All I know is that he came ashore on a great turtle," he says. "How he did it I can't imagine. But he also brought a diving-suit. Would you like me to show you where it is?" They hurry away while the old Professor buttons up his blazer, takes Rupert on his shoulder, and trots away to find Mrs Bear. When she comes in sight he puts him down and the little bear runs to greet his Mummy. Like all the others she can hardly believe that it is really Rupert.

When she has got over the first shock Mrs Bear hugs Rupert and holds him close. "This settles it," she breathes shakily. "That must positively be your last adventure. Never will I let you go with that terrible old man again!" "Oh *please*, Mummy," Rupert begs. "It was all *my* fault. He told me not to put that diving-suit on and I disobeyed him. And look, I've brought a wonderful present from Father Neptune all for you! Do let's go back to our rooms and see what's in it."

RUPERT OPENS THE PACKAGE

He tells his tale, while all admire
The gorgeous shells that glow like fire.

They all walk back towards the shore,
Then Rupert meets the Scout once more.

"What was it like beneath the sea?"
Says Geoffrey, when he's asked to tea.

Smiles Mummy, "We must always keep
These lovely treasures from the deep."

Soon the seaweed package is opened and they are all dazzled by the sparkling, glowing colours of the treasures from the bottom of the ocean. "Father Neptune said that you shouldn't search wrecks for a silly thing like gold," says Rupert. And he tells the whole story. At last the Professor has to leave, and Mrs Bear and Rupert go with him as far as the beach. "If Rupert hadn't disobeyed me I shouldn't be alive to hear that wonderful tale!" he says in farewell. As the Professor goes the Boy Scout appears. "Oh look, here's Geoffrey," Rupert cries. "I promised that he should hear my story too." So Mrs Bear prepares tea and the adventure has to be described again. Then Rupert looks wistful. "You didn't mean it when you said that was to be my last adventure, did you, Mummy?" he says. "The Professor invents such lovely things and, you never know, I may be able to help him again when his ideas go wrong!" Mrs Bear sighs deeply. "We'll see," she murmurs. THE END

TIGERLILY'S PARTY

Rupert and his friends are at a moonlight party in Tigerlily's mysterious garden. Suddenly Tigerlily waves her wand and all except Rupert disappear. "Oh dear, they've vanished!" he cries, "where have they gone?" "They've not gone! They're still here," laughs Tigerlily. She is quite right. Bill Badger is there, so are Algy Pug, Podgy Pig, Edward Trunk, Willie Whiskers, Rex and Reggie Rabbit and Freddy and Ferdy Fox. Also Tigerlily's two cats. Can you see where they all are?

RUPERT and the
RAINBOW

**Telling how Rupert
with the help of the
clerk of the weather
gives a surprise
birthday present.**

RUPERT SEES THE RAINBOW

"Oh good!" cries Rupert Bear with glee,
"This note invites me out to tea."

To buy a present Rupert goes,
When suddenly it rains and blows.

So Rupert thinks, "I'll shelter here,"
Then Edward Trunk he sees quite near.

"Thanks for your letter," Rupert cries,
"Your party is a grand surprise."

"Look, Mummy," cries Rupert, "the postman's brought me a letter inviting me to Edward Trunk's birthday party next Thursday. May I go?" "Yes, of course you may," says Mrs Bear, "and you'd better go over to the village at once to see if you can find him a present." So off he runs. Soon he is surprised by a flock of birds flying before a sudden squall. "This is odd," he thinks. "Surely there should not be sunshine and rain both together."

Rupert shelters under a big tree while the squall passes and a lovely rainbow follows. While he is gazing at this a little figure passes near to him. "Why, it's Edward himself," he says. "Hi, Edward! Thanks for your letter. I'm coming to your party. What's that thing you're carrying?" "It's the party that's worrying me," says Edward. "I've borrowed this garden umbrella from Granny Goat in case the weather's bad."

RUPERT MEETS THE SQUIRREL

Poor Edward hopes it will not rain,
Then says he must be off again.

As Rupert slowly walks along,
A friendly squirrel asks, "What's wrong?"

"Oh dear," says Rupert with a sigh,
"I wish I knew what I could buy."

The squirrel says, "Why don't you ask
The owl to help you with your task?"

"I'm determined to have the party in the open air," continues Edward, "so I'll have to borrow more umbrellas and things. You can't trust the weather these days. I must hurry now. Goodbye." And off he trudges. "Poor old Edward," thinks Rupert, "that party's getting on his mind." He moves slowly through a patch of woodland wondering what present he can give him, when a little voice pipes, "Why so solemn, Rupert?"

Gazing up sharply Rupert sees his pal, the squirrel, peeping down, so he scrambles up into the branches beside him. "I wonder if you can help me," he says. "I want to give Edward a really nice present. Can you think of anything a little elephant would like?" "Oh dear, I'm no good at thinking!" says the squirrel. "Why not ask the wise old owl? He's frightfully clever and he lives in the middle of that clump of trees."

RUPERT ASKS FOR ADVICE

"I will!" the little bear agrees,
And hurries off towards the trees.

The bushes are so thick and tall,
It's hard to get through them at all.

And when, at last, he does get through,
A grass snakes tell him what to do.

High in the tree climbs Rupert Bear,
And finds the old owl sitting there.

Thanking the squirrel for his idea Rupert descends from the tree and trots up the slope to the clump of trees at the top. Then he meets a problem, for the bushes are so thick that he can only push in a few yards. He walks right round the clump but can find no way to the middle of it. "I *will* find that wise old owl!" he says, and, kneeling down, he shuts his eyes and starts to force his way through the undergrowth.

Opening his eyes Rupert finds himself in a clearing and facing a large grass-snake. "Oh please, is this the wise old owl's tree?" he asks. "Yes, go straight up," says the snake. And in a few minutes the little bear is explaining to the surprised bird why he has come. "Edward's worried about the weather and I do want to give him something to cheer him up," he says. "You're so clever. Can you suggest a present for him?"

RUPERT IS DISAPPOINTED

The owl seems rather cross today,
But hears what Rupert has to say.

"You want a fine day!" he replies,
Then suddenly away he flies.

"The owl is clever," says the snake,
"He never makes a bad mistake."

Poor Rupert walks on feeling glum;
What present can he buy his chum?

The wise old owl closes his eyes and looks bored. "Oh, please don't go to sleep!" begs Rupert, "I want you to think hard and help me." "Think? There's nothing to think about," says the bird peevishly. "It's all too simple. You say Edward's worried about the weather? Very well then, why not give him a FINE DAY?" And he flies out of the tree so suddenly that Rupert topples off his branch and nearly has a bad fall.

Rupert saves himself from a nasty tumble by clinging to another branch and then, feeling very shaken, he carefully climbs down. "Well, did the owl do what you wished?" asks the grass-snake. "No," says Rupert indignantly. "What he said sounded silly to me." "Steady on," says the snake, "the wise old owl never makes a mistake." But the little bear pushes his way out of the clump again and wanders rather moodily down the slope.

RUPERT GETS A SURPRISE

When Rupert meets the owl once more,
He seems more friendly than before.

He says, "Your friend shall have his day,
This little bird will lead the way."

They climb a very rocky hill,
And then the little bird stands still.

The large bird Rupert's come to seek
Is perched upon the highest peak.

Rupert does not raise his eyes from the ground until a voice beside him makes him stop. The wise old owl has settled on a post and a smaller bird is fluttering around. "Why did you leave my tree, little bear?" says the owl. "I have arranged for you to have your wish and to give Edward a fine day. Follow this messenger-bird and do as he tells you." "I say, thanks awfully!" gasps Rupert. He is quite bewildered, but he follows the little bird at his best speed.

After passing through another patch of woodland Rupert finds himself being led up a steep and very rocky hill. "Please, where are we going?" he puffs. The little bird stops. "I have orders to take you to see the Clerk of the Weather. He may be able to arrange for a fine day for Edward's party," he pipes. So Rupert has to climb right to the top until he is nearly in the clouds. Then he sees an enormous bird standing on a near-by peak.

Rupert and the Rainbow

RUPERT IS CARRIED AWAY

The bird swoops down on Rupert Bear,
Then takes him swiftly through the air.

So high they go into the sky,
For through the rainbow they must fly.

On, on they fly, so very fast,
And reach their journey's end at last.

Here, in this house, so far away,
The weather man works hard all day.

After flying across to the other peak the small bird returns to Rupert and tells him to lie down flat. Next moment, the little bear feels himself gripped by powerful talons and swung high into the air. "Don't be frightened," pipes the little voice, "this is a carrier-bird. He'll take you where you want to go." The strong wings mount higher. "You can never find the Clerk of the Weather unless you fly through a rainbow first," says the great bird.

After flying straight through a rainbow which had appeared to the north, the carrier-bird makes for an extra thick cloud and, to his amazement, Rupert sees that a strange house covered with queer gadgets is nestling in the top of it. The bird hovers near a balcony just as a fussy little man pops his head over the edge. "Bless my soul, if it isn't a little bear!" he says. "Dear, dear, how very odd! But don't hang about there. Come in, come in, come in."

RUPERT MAKES A REQUEST

When Rupert makes his strange request,
The queer man says, "I'll do my best."

"How odd this is," thinks Rupert Bear,
"With all these gadgets everywhere."

Inside his office, once again
The Clerk asks Rupert to explain.

"Yes," says the Clerk, "that is all right;
Next Thursday shall be fine and bright."

Rupert is landed gently on the balcony. Then the giant bird flies away. "Please, are you the Clerk of the Weather?" asks the little bear. "Could you give me a fine day for next Thursday?" The Clerk stares. "Fine? Every day's fine for somebody," he says; "a rainy day's fine for ducks Rund a windy day's fine for kites and sailing ships and a frosty day's fine for penguins. Come to my office and explain." And he marches Rupert off past some of his queer gadgets.

In the office Rupert explains that all he wants is a sunny day for Edward's party. "D'you mean to say you've come all this way to get your friend a sunny day? You're very brave!" says the Clerk, peering at him closely. He turns to his books and his charts. "H'm, ha, yes, yes," he murmurs, "there's no reason why Nutwood shouldn't have sunshine next Thursday, no reason at all; quite a good idea in fact, yes, yes. I'll write out the Order at once."

RUPERT GETS THE ORDERS

To Nutwood now he must send word,
And so he calls the little bird.

"Oh, thank you!" Rupert cries. "And now
I have to get back home somehow."

"That's simple," is the Clerk's reply;
"This magic vapour we will try."

Now Rupert gleams from top to toe,
As to the roof-tops now they go.

Taking the Order for a fine Thursday the Clerk of the Weather gives it to the small messenger-bird who has been flying inquisitively around. "Take this to my Deputy-Assistant-Section-Controller of the Nutwood Sub-area," he says. "There, little bear, that has settled what you wanted." Rupert smiles, then he pauses. "Thank you very much," he says, "but how am I to get back? The carrier-bird has gone and now you've sent the messenger-bird away!"

The Clerk of the Weather thinks hard for a moment. "Don't worry, little bear," he says, "I'll send you back by rainbow." Taking him into a small room he stands him in front of a small machine and sprays him with shining vapour that tingles and makes Rupert giggle. "There, that's rainbow mixture," says the Clerk. "Now you can ride a rainbow and won't go through it!" Then he leads Rupert up to the very topmost part of the building.

RUPERT RIDES THE RAINBOW

The Clerk says, "Watch and I'll explain,
Just how I mix the sun and rain."

"Oh look!" cries Rupert in delight,
"This rainbow is a lovely sight."

The Clerk tells Rupert what to do,
"just walk on top; you won't fall through."

Down, down he slides, so very fast,
And lands in Nutwood lake, at last.

At the top of the building the Clerk of the Weather gets to work on two of his strange machines. "For a rainbow we must have sunshine and rain together," he murmurs. He turns a wheel and pulls a handle and peers over the parapet anxiously. Rupert looks over, too, and sees a gorgeous rainbow coming nearer until it is exactly underneath him. "Here you are, little bear," says the Clerk, "you can get out and walk on that. Just try."

Very gingerly Rupert steps over the parapet and to his amazement finds he can walk along the rainbow. "It must be because I am coated with that rainbow mixture," he thinks. He hears the Clerk's voice behind him saying, "Don't be frightened, Rupert, you won't come to any harm." When he reaches the curve his feet slip and he finds himself sliding down the rainbow, down and down till he lands "splash" in the edge of Nutwood lake.

RUPERT KEEPS HIS PROMISE

When Rupert scrambles from the lake,
He laughs and gives himself a shake.

He soon meets Edward Trunk again,
As he is sheltering from the rain.

Next day, the rainbow is still there,
"It will be fine!" laughs Rupert Bear.

And so it proves that he is right,
For all day long the sun shines bright.

Rupert is not hurt but, feeling breathless and frightened, he scrambles out of the lake and gives himself a shake. To his delight all the water flies off him in a shower of little drops. Rain starts as he runs towards Nutwood and he finds Edward sheltering under a tree. "Hi, Edward, you needn't worry any more," he cries. "I'm giving you a sunny day on Thursday!" He looks so strange, shining with rainbow mixture, that Edward is quite speechless.

Next morning Rupert's rainbow mixture has worn off, but there is a rainbow in the sky, and some of the little people look anxious. "You needn't worry," says the little bear, "this weather will all have gone by Thursday." And, sure enough, the party takes place in brilliant sunshine. "I can't imagine how you did it, Rupert," declares Edward, "but this gift of a fine, sunny day is quite the most unexpected and wonderful birthday present I've ever had!" THE END

RUPERT
and the
Apple Trees

John Harrold.

RUPERT'S PAL GETS A WARNING

One morning Rupert hears a cry,
"It's Podgy calling me, but why?"

"Stop!" Farmer Brown calls. "Come back here!"
"Help!" Podgy wails. "He's getting near!"

"Podgy!" cries Farmer Brown. "I'm sure
You stole some fruit and broke the law!"

"No!" Podgy wails. "It wasn't me!
I didn't climb a single tree . . ."

One autumn morning, Rupert is walking across Nutwood Common when he suddenly hears somebody calling his name . . . "It's Podgy!" he thinks, "I wonder what's wrong? He looks as if he might need help!" "Rupert!" gasps Podgy. "Run for your life! The farmer's coming! He chased me all the way from the orchard!" Sure enough, Rupert spots an angry Farmer Brown, running after Podgy as fast as he can. "Come back here, Podgy Pig!" he bellows. "I want a word with you . . ."

Farmer Brown is so cross that he hardly seems to notice Rupert. "Podgy!" he cries. "I've had enough of your greedy scrumping. Any more and I'll have to have words with Constable Growler!" "But I wasn't!" protested Podgy. "I only took a short cut . . ." "To *look* at the apples, I suppose!" growls the farmer. "One of you lads has been scrumping in my orchard, that's for sure. I found a branch broken off the oldest tree and twigs all over the ground. It's got to stop, or there'll be trouble!"

RUPERT HEARS PODGY'S TALE

*"I didn't have a chance to take
His fruit! It's all a big mistake!"*

*"If Podgy wasn't scrumping then
The apple thief might strike again . . ."*

*When Rupert gets home, Mr Bear
Is looking at the apples there . . .*

*"There isn't time this afternoon,
But we should pick our harvest soon!"*

"What a fuss!" says Podgy as Farmer Brown turns on his heel and marches off. "I wouldn't mind, but I really *haven't* been scrumping apples! I was just about to start when Farmer Brown saw me . . ." Rupert warns his chum to stay out of the orchard until things have calmed down. "Don't worry!" says Podgy. "I won't even go near the farm for the next few days!" "If Podgy hasn't been scrumping apples, I wonder who has?" thinks Rupert. "Probably Freddy and Ferdy! I'd better warn them, too . . ."

When Rupert gets home, Mr Bear is out in the garden looking at his apple trees . . . "It's nearly time to harvest our crop!" he declares. "Perhaps you could give me a hand at the weekend?" Rupert agrees and remembers how delicious home-grown apples always taste. "That's because they're so fresh!" smiles his father. "Come on, you two!" calls Mrs Bear. "It's time for tea. I'd better get my bottling jars ready if you're about to start picking apples . . ."

RUPERT SEES STRANGE LIGHTS

When Rupert goes to bed that night
He spots two tiny points of light . . .

"They look like lanterns," Ruper blinks.
"I'm sure I saw them move!" he thinks.

As he gets closer, Rupert sees
Two figures in the apple trees . . .

"Look out! Calls one as he gets near.
"We're not alone! There's someone here . . ."

Later in the evening, as Rupert gets ready for bed, he looks out into the garden and notices something strange. "I can see lights in one of the apple trees!" he gasps. "They look just like fireflies . . ." Hurrying downstairs, he opens the back door and steps outside. The lights are still there, glowing in the darkness like tiny lanterns. "How peculiar!" thinks Rupert as he walks silently towards the tree. "The lights are still moving. They seem to be going from branch to branch . . ."

As Rupert gets nearer to the apple trees he sees that the moving lights *are* tiny lanterns, held by Elf-like creatures with pointed hats . . . "They're looking for something!" he thinks. "I wonder what it can be?" Creeping forward, Rupert reaches the first tree and peers up at one of the little men. Before he can say anything, the Elf spins round with a cry of alarm. "Jonathan!" he calls. "There's somebody here . . ." "Don't worry!" says Rupert. "I'm sorry if I startled you . . ."

50

RUPERT MEETS THE PIPPINS

Who can the little green men be?
Why are they in the apple tree?

"We're Pippins!" cries the first. "We find
Gold apples of a special kind . . ."

"Each tree bears one gold fruit. We know
That its pips are the best to grow . . ."

As Rupert talks, the little pair
Hear someone call – It's Mrs Bear!

Rupert is puzzled by the little men. At first, they look like Imps or Autumn Elves, but as he looks more closely he sees that they are dressed quite differently, in shades of green from head to toe . . . "Who are you?" he asks. "I hope you haven't been raiding Farmer Brown's orchard!" "No!" laughs the little man. "We're Pippins, not scrumpers! My name's Bramley and he's called Jonathan . . ." "What are you looking for?" asks Rupert. "A golden apple!" calls Jonathan. "There's one on every tree, you know!"

To Rupert's amazement, the Pippins say they collect golden apples from every tree they visit. "They have the best pips for planting!" explains Jonathan. "We use them all to bring on new trees . . ." "I've never noticed golden apples before," says Rupert. "No!" nods Bramley. "We normally pick them early." "This year's different!" his companion sighs. "Someone else has been gathering golden apples too! Farmer Brown's orchard is almost bare!" Just then, the door opens and Mrs Bear calls Rupert's name . . .

51

RUPERT INVESTIGATES

"Who's there?" asks Mrs Bear, but then
The Pippins have both gone again . . .

"Come in!" she smiles. "You sleepy head!
It's time you were tucked up in bed . . ."

Next morning, Rupert hurries out
To see if Pippins are about . . .

As Rupert nears the orchard he
Spots Freddy, climbing up a tree!

"Do I hear voices?" asks Mrs Bear. "Who are you talking to?" "Pippins!" says Rupert. "I found them in our apple tree . . ." He turns back to show Bramley and Jonathan to his mother but the glowing lanterns have gone and the garden is completely deserted. "Come in!" she smiles. "It's too late to play games outside now." "But they *were* here," gasps Rupert. "I saw them, really! Collecting golden apples from each tree . . ." "Rupert!" says Mrs Bear. "There'll be plenty of time to play tomorrow!"

Next morning, Rupert decides to go and ask Odmedod the scarecrow if *he* knows anything about the Pippins . . . "He's bound to have seen them gathering apples in Farmer Brown's orchard!" he thinks. "I wonder if he knows where they live?" On the way to Trees farm, Rupert suddenly notices somebody climbing a tree in the lower orchard. "Freddy Fox!" he blinks. "And there's Ferdy, waiting down below. So they *have* been scrumping apples, while poor old Podgy got the blame!"

RUPERT WARNS THE FOXES

*"Look out!" warns Rupert. "Hurry down.
You'll both be caught by Farmer Brown!"*

*"Don't worry! He can have the rest –
These yellow apples taste the best!"*

*Just then, the Foxes hear a yell –
The farmer's spotted them as well . . .*

*"Run!" Ferdy calls. The Foxes flee
As Farmer Brown shouts angrily.*

Rupert scrambles into the orchard and runs across to warn the Foxes. "Farmer Brown's on the warpath!" he gasps. "There'll be trouble if he spots you scrumping apples . . ." "He won't mind!" laughs Ferdy. "We're only picking *one* apple from each tree!" "These yellowy ones taste much better than all the others," says Freddy. "I've never noticed them before, but they're really delicious!" "Yellow?" blinks Rupert. "But those are the golden apples the Pippins need!"

"Pippins?" asks Freddy. "Who are they? They can't have our apples anyway!" Rupert is about to explain, when he hears an angry cry . . . "Farmer Brown!" gasps Ferdy, dropping his sack. "Run for it!" shouts his brother. The pair take to their heels, with the farmer in hot pursuit. "He didn't see me!" thinks Rupert. "I must have been hidden behind this bush." Keeping out of sight, he decides to wait till the farmer has gone. By his side lies the Fox brothers' sack, filled with golden apples . . .

RUPERT SAVES THE SPECIAL APPLES

"The Foxes' apples!" Rupert blinks.
"They've left them all behind!" he thinks . . .

Just then he hears a Pippin call,
"Phew! That was close! I saw it all!"

The Pippin smiles to find out how
The yellow fruit's been gathered now . . .

"We'll take it to the Nursery!
I'll lead the way. You follow me!"

As Farmer Brown disappears after the Foxes, Rupert picks up the sack of apples and wonders what to do next. "Hello!" calls a voice. "That was a close run thing! You're lucky the farmer didn't see you!" Looking up, Rupert spots a little figure peering down from the branches of a nearby tree. "One of the Pippins!" he blinks. "That's right!" smiles the little man. "I'm Jonathan. We met last night. I've come to have a final look in Farmer Brown's orchard . . ."

When Rupert explains how the Foxes have been gathering golden apples, the Pippin is overjoyed. "They've done my work for me!" he laughs. "There are enough here to grow a hundred trees. All we have to do is get them to the Nursery . . ." "Nursery?" asks Rupert. "Yes!" says the Pippin. "It's where we grow new trees. After all you've done to help, I'm sure the others won't mind if you come too." Intrigued to find out more, Rupert follows Jonathan through the trees, across the orchard.

54

RUPERT SEES A SECRET DOOR

*"This way!" the Pippin calls. "I'll show
You something only Pippins know . . ."*

*"A door!" blinks Rupert. "Now I see . . .
Each Pippin has a special key!"*

*"Like Imps and Elves we move around
Through secret tunnels underground!"*

*"You'll soon see where the others are!"
The Pippin calls. "It isn't far . . ."*

Leading Rupert to the edge of the orchard, the Pippin stops suddenly by a tangle of bushes. "I'm about to show you a secret!" he says. "Stay close behind me and keep down low . . ." Pushing his way forward, Jonathan reveals a tiny doorway in the wall, completely hidden by a mass of leaves. "It's a short cut!" he smiles. "Elves and Imps use it too, but Farmer Brown doesn't even know it's here!" taking a key from his pocket, the Pippin unlocks the door and pushes it open for Rupert to enter . . .

On the other side of the door, Rupert is surprised to find a rocky tunnel, leading underground . . . "I thought we were going to another orchard," he blinks. "We are!" laughs his guide. "This is a special pathway between our orchard and Farmer Brown's." "I wonder how far it goes?" thinks Rupert as he follows the Pippin. "I've never really thought about the far side of the orchard. I suppose we'll come out somewhere near the middle of Nutwood Forest . . ."

RUPERT REACHES AN ORCHARD

"We're nearly there now! Can you see?
A glimpse of daylight! Follow me . . ."

"Another orchard!" Rupert cries.
*"It's **full** of Pippins! What a size . . ."*

"Look, everybody! We've come back
With yellow apples in our sack!"

"The Apple Cart! Let's see if he
Will take us to the Nursery . . ."

Carrying the sack of golden apples, Rupert follows Jonathan along a winding tunnel that seems to go on and on for miles . . . "Nearly there!" calls the Pippin cheerfully. "There! You can see the end. We won't be long now!" Emerging into the sunshine, Rupert is amazed to see a huge orchard, filled with Pippins, all busily picking apples from the trees. "Harvest time!" says Jonathan. "It's a busy month for us! Follow me and I'll take you to see the Nurseries . . ."

The other Pippins are astonished to see an unexpected visitor. "We've brought the golden apples from Farmer Brown's!" explains Jonathan. "They're needed in the Nursery straightaway." "The Nursery?" asks one of the harvesters. "You're just in time! There's an Apple Cart about to leave with a full load. Hurry along and you can hitch a ride!" Jonathan runs to a grassy clearing where a horse and cart stand waiting. "Hello, there!" he calls. "Don't go yet! We'd like to come too . . ."

RUPERT MEETS THE CHIEF GARDENER

The cart moves off and Rupert sees
Some buildings set among the trees.

The Pippin hurries off to tell
The Gardener that all is well . . .

The Pippins' Chief is pleased at all
The golden apples – "What a haul!"

"Please stay for lunch and let us show
You what we do, before you go . . ."

To Rupert's delight, the driver of the Apple Cart turns out to be Bramley, the other Pippin he met in the garden. "Climb up!" he smiles. "Everyone *will* be pleased you've got the goldens!" As the cart trundles across the orchard, Rupert spots a cluster of buildings grouped around some glass-houses . . . "The Nursery!" announces Jonathan. He hops down and hurries off to tell the Chief Gardener the news. "Old Laxton!" nods Bramley. "He's in charge of all our new trees . . ."

The Chief Gardener is delighted to see Rupert's sack of golden apples. "Just what we need!" he cries. Each pip will grow into a little seedling and, in time, there'll be plenty of new trees to keep the orchards going . . ." When he hears how he has helped the Pippins, the Chief invites Rupert to stay for a while and have a closer look at the Nursery. "Jonathan will show you round," he says. "The other Pippins are just about to have lunch. Why don't you two go and join them?"

RUPERT HAS A TOFFEE APPLE

The Pippins' menu shows that they
Eat apple dishes every day!

"Each apple's different! Our cooks know
What's best for every type we grow . . ."

"There's one more thing you ought to see . . .
Our toffee apple factory!"

"The ones that we don't eat are sold
To shops, like Nutwood's!" Rupert's told . . .

Rupert follows Jonathan into the Pippins' canteen. When he looks at the menu, he sees that everything on it is made from apples! "They're our favourite food!" says Jonathan. "It's amazing what you can do with apples. We grow everything here – from Pearmains to pimpernels!" "Toffee-apples!" laughs Rupert. "My friend Podgy loves those!" "Try one!" says the Pippin. "They're from this morning's batch. I'll show you how they're made, if you like. The toffee's a special recipe we invented ourselves!"

When Rupert has finished lunch, his guide leads him along a path towards another building. The air is suddenly filled with a strong, sweet smell which wafts towards them. "Toffee!" smiles Jonathan. Rupert follows him into a busy kitchen, where Pippins are dipping apples into a bubbling vat, then standing them to cool on trays. "We make a fresh batch every day," he explains. "Those we don't eat are packaged up and sold to shops. Your friend Podgy must be one of our best customers!"

RUPERT GETS AN INVITATION

As Rupert walks along he sees
A picture of some apple trees . . .

"Wassailing's when we stay out late –
Come too and help us celebrate!"

The Pippins wait till twilight, then
Set out towards the trees again . . .

"Stay close to us and use your light!"
Says Bramley. "Don't get lost at night!"

As Rupert is taken to see how juice is made at the apple press, he catches sight of a poster on the wall . . . "Grand Wassailing!" he reads. "That's tonight!" says Jonathan. "We're going to water the trees with a special tonic. It's a sort of thank-you for all the apples they've given us. We sing songs as well and celebrate the autumn's harvest." "What fun!" laughs Rupert. "Do you go to Farmer Brown's orchard?" "Of course!" nods Jonathan. "You can come too! We go when it's dark, so that nobody sees . . ."

The Pippins spend the rest of the afternoon getting ready for the Grand Wassailing . . . "We need enough tonic for the whole orchard!" explains Jonathan. "It only takes a few drops for each tree but there are hundreds to visit." As darkness falls, the Pippins light their lanterns and hand one to Rupert. "You'll need this!" says Bramley. "It's easy to get lost in the dark, so make sure you stay close to us." "Time to go!" calls Jonathan. "Wassailers join the Round!"

RUPERT SINGS WITH THE PIPPINS

The Pippins all stand in a ring
And wait until it's time to sing . . .

A horn blows and they all begin –
"Hurrah!" calls Rupert, joining in . . .

Now Rupert knows the Pippins' song,
He sings it as they march along . . .

"Our last tree! Now we've done them all
It's time to make another call . . ."

As Rupert joins the Pippins, he finds them gathered round the first tree in a big circle. "Ready, everyone?" asks Jonathan. Bramley nods and gestures to a third Pippin who blows a long, loud note on his horn. The others start to sing as Bramley sprays the tree with tonic. "Here's to thee, good apple tree. We thank you for the fruit we store. Caps full, sacks full. Holla! Holla! Hurrah!" Rupert laughs then joins them in a final chorus. "Holla! Holla! Hurrah!"

Moving from apple tree to apple tree, the Pippins spray each one with tonic and sing the same song over and over again. Before long, Rupert knows all the words and can join in from start to finish. "Caps full, sacks full. Holla! Holla! Hurrah!" When the Wassailers have been round the whole orchard, Jonathan leads them towards the clump of bushes which marks the start of the tunnel back to Nutwood. "This way, everyone!" he calls. "Our night's work isn't over yet!"

RUPERT JOINS A PROCESSION

"This way! There's still a lot to do!
We spray all Farmer Brown's trees too . . ."

"What fun!" thinks Rupert. "Now I know
What makes all Farmer Brown's trees grow!"

The Pippins march from tree to tree
And sing to each one cheerfully.

Then, finally, there's one last flask
Of tonic for a special task . . .

With their tiny lanterns shimmering in the gloom, the Pippins set off along the rocky tunnel towards Farmer Brown's orchard. "If only he knew!" laughs Rupert. "I am glad you asked me to come wassailing too!" "You're welcome!" says Jonathan. "If it hadn't been for your help, we would have lost Nutwood's golden apples and been short of seedlings to replant!" At the end of the tunnel Jonathan opens the door and leads the band of wassailers to the first of Farmer Brown's trees . . .

In Farmer Brown's orchard the Pippins sing their Wassailing song, blow their horn and spray tonic on every tree. "It will help them through the winter," explains Bramley. "Frost and fog, rain and snow, and hardly a ray of sunshine till Spring arrives! Poor trees! I feel chilly just thinking about it!" When the tour of the orchard has ended, the Pippins still have one bottle of tonic left over . . . "That's for our final call!" smiles Jonathan. "It's somewhere you should recognise!"

RUPERT'S FATHER IS MYSTIFIED

"My house!" laughs Rupert. "Now I see,
You've saved the last wassail for me!"

The Pippins start to sing their song
Then stop abruptly – something's wrong!

It's Mr Bear! "Who's there?" he cries
And takes the Pippins by surprise . . .

"They've gone!" "Yes!" Rupert smiles. "But I
Can tell you what they do – and why . . ."

Rupert marches off along the lane, then laughs when he realises where the Pippins are going next. "My house!" he blinks. "That's right!" says Jonathan. "We've come to sing to *your* trees!" Handing Rupert the last bottle of tonic, he leads the Pippins in a rousing chorus while Rupert works the spray . . . They have just finished when the garden is suddenly flooded with light from the kitchen. "Somebody's coming!" gasps Bramley. "They must have seen the glint of our lanterns!"

"Hello!" calls Rupert's father. "You're out very late! What were all those lights I saw? Is there somebody here?" "There was!" smiles Rupert. "They've gone now, I'm afraid. Pippins don't like being seen . . ." "Pippins?" blinks Mr Bear. "Apple Elves!" says Rupert. "We've been out wassailing!" "Really!" laughs his father, then spots Rupert's bottle. "Tree tonic!" beams Rupert. "Let's go inside and I'll tell you all about it . . ."

RUPERT'S FOLD-A-BOWL

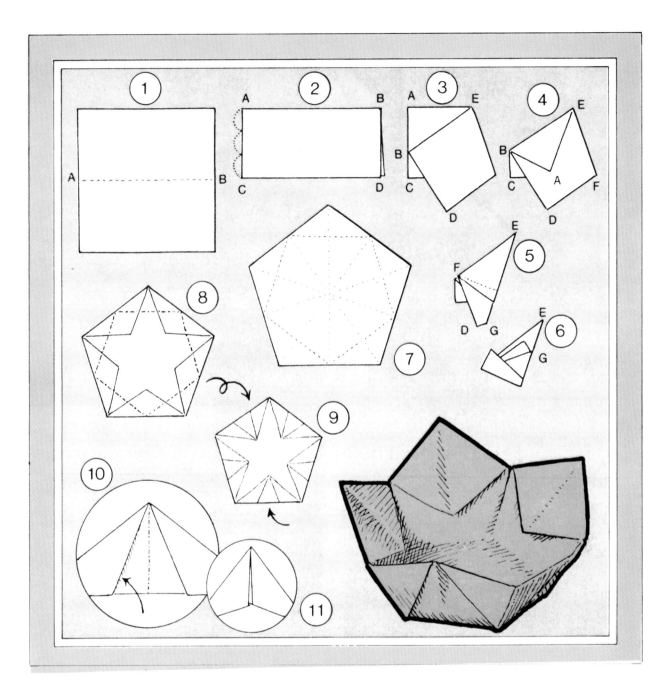

This five-point bowl from Hong Kong was made by the expert, Dr Philip Shen. You might make one or two to hold sweets or crisps at a party.

To get the five-sided piece of paper you need, take a fairly big square (fig. 1). Fold it in half along the line AB (fig. 2). Bring down B to a point exactly one third the way up side CA (fig. 3). Take A down, making the fold along EB (fig. 4). Now carry F across, creasing the line EA. EF should now lie along EB so that F and B are very nearly touching (fig. 5). Take G up on the line EG so that the new crease is the dotted line to F (fig. 6).

Press and return to fig. 5. Cut along the crease. Now E is the centre of a pentagon with a crease

from each point to the centre of the opposite side (fig. 7). Fold each point towards the middle so that the new creases go *exactly* to the centre of the edge on each side (fig. 8). Turn the shape over and do the same again (fig. 9).

The arrow shows a sharp triangle in the middle of a side, drawn larger in fig. 10. Lift the point then pinch the middle of the triangle so that it rises and pulls together the two nearer edges. Now tuck the pinched centre under either of the edges you have pulled together (fig. 11), press firmly and bend the point back into position. (If this is slightly tricky, ask Daddy's or Mummy's help.) Repeat with all five sides. There's your bowl!

RUPERT and

The post arrives one autumn day –
"An envelope – what does it say?"

One autumn morning, Rupert has just finished breakfast when he hears the post arrive . . . "It's an invitation!" he cries. "Ottoline's having a Halloween party and everyone is invited to come in fancy dress." "What fun!" says Rupert's father. "I remember bobbing for apples when I was a lad! We used to have lanterns too!" he chuckles. "You can make one if you like and take it to Ottoline's party to light the way . . ."

the Pumpkin Pie

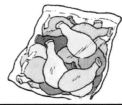

"To Rupert Bear – from Ottoline!
Please join us all on Halloween . . ."

"A pumpkin lantern would be fun!"
Says Mr Bear. "I'll buy you one . . ."

Rupert is so keen to make a lantern that his father agrees they can go and buy a pumpkin straightaway. "I saw a big pile in Mr Chimp's shop," he says. "I hope there are still a few left . . . When the pair arrive, they find Bill Badger and his mother are already there. "Hello, Rupert!" cries Bill. "I've come to buy a pumpkin to make a lantern for Ottoline's party . . ." "So have I!" laughs Rupert. "I hope that isn't the last one."

Rupert arrives to find Bill's Mum
Buying a pumpkin for his chum . . .

RUPERT MAKES A LANTERN

*"I know!" says Mrs Badger. "I
can make us all a pumpkin pie!"*

*"Good luck, you two! It's quite a task
To turn a pumpkin to a mask . . ."*

*The pals start working carefully –
"That's right – save the inside for me . . ."*

*They start with eyes – then cut out rows
Of jagged teeth and make a nose . . .*

Luckily for Rupert, Mr Chimp produces a second pumpkin, so the pals can have one each. "If Rupert comes back to our house you can both make lanterns together!" says Mrs Badger. "And I can make a pumpkin pie at the same time . . ." "Good idea!" laughs Mr Bear. "Then nothing will be wasted. Perhaps they could take your pie to the party too." The delighted chums set off across the common towards Bill's house. "See you later!" calls Mr Bear. "Have fun making the lanterns."

At Bill's house the two chums settle down to start work on their lanterns . . . "Cut off the tops first, then scoop out both pumpkins," says Mrs Badger. "When you've finished that, you can cut faces in the hollow shells." The pals carefully empty the pumpkins into a bowl, then start work on a pair of frightening faces. "Very good!" smiles Mrs Badger. "Now I'll find you both candles to go inside. You'll need some string too, for making handles, then you can carry the lanterns along."

RUPERT'S COSTUME IS READY

"Thanks, Bill!" calls Rupert. "We can light
Our way with these, tomorrow night!"

"Well done!" says Mrs Bear. "Now you
Will need to choose a costume too . . ."

"I'll help you too!" says Mr Bear.
"You'll need a pointed hat to wear . . ."

"A wizard costume!" Rupert tells
His mother he's made up some spells . . .

Rupert and Bill are thrilled with their lanterns. "They'll look even better when it's dark!" says Rupert. "I can't wait to show mine to everyone else." Mr Bear is pleased too. "Well done!" he says. "Just the thing for tomorrow night." Remembering Ottoline's party, Rupert asks his mother if she will help him make a costume. "Of course!" she laughs. "What would you like to go as?" Rupert can't decide. "An Egyptian mummy? A skeleton?" Finally, he has a good idea . . .

The next day, Rupert's parents both help him make a costume . . . "Going as a wizard is a splendid idea!" says Mr Bear. "I agree!" says Rupert's mother. "With a pointed hat and star-spangled gown you'll really look the part!" When everything is ready, Rupert puts on his costume and chants a spell, just like the Chinese Conjurer. "My wand shall summon everyone, to Ottoline's – to join the fun!" "Very good!" laughs Mr Bear. "Goodness! There's someone at the door already . . ."

RUPERT'S PAL ARRIVES

"Good gracious!" Rupert's father cries
*When Bill arrives in **his** disguise . . .*

"Count Dracula" has brought a pie
For all the party guests to try . . .

The chums set off – their lanterns glow
And light the pathway as they go . . .

Then, suddenly, the pals both see
A stranger. "Look! Who can it be?"

As Mr Bear opens the door he gives a cry of surprise and starts back in alarm. "Hello, Mr Bear!" laughs Bill. "Sorry if I scared you! I'm going to the party as Count Dracula . . ." As well as his lantern, Bill is also carrying Mrs Badger's pumpkin pie, which everyone gathers round to admire. "What a nice idea to take it with you," says Rupert's mother. "I'll say!" nods Mr Bear. "It looks delicious!" "Time we were going!" says Bill. "I hope my outfit isn't *too* creepy!"

"Goodbye!" calls Mrs Bear as the pals set off with their pumpkin lanterns glowing. "It's just as well you've got something with you to light the way . . ." Darkness falls as the pair reach the edge of the common and all they can see are the shadows of bushes and trees. "I say!" whispers Bill. "There's someone coming towards us." "You're right!" gasps Rupert. "I wonder who it can be?" "Good evening!" booms a deep voice. "Is this the way to Nutwood's haunted Manor?"

RUPERT AND HIS PALS ARE ROBBED

The "monster" chuckles as he comes
Towards the pair of startled chums . . .

"It's Algy Pug!" laughs Bill. "Trust you
To make a scary costume too . . ."

Two "highwaymen" confront the three –
The Fox twins – hiding by a tree . . .

"Hands up!" calls Freddy. "Trick or treat!"
"We're after booty we can eat . . ."

As the lumbering figure approaches, Bill and Rupert are both convinced he looks oddly familiar . . . "Algy Pug!" laughs Rupert. "Hello!" chuckles his pal. "How do you like my costume? I made the helmet out of cardboard, then dressed up in one of my father's old coats." "Excellent!" says Bill. "You really had me fooled! I'd forgotten how we used to think Nutwood Manor was haunted. That was before Ottoline arrived, of course. There won't be any *real* ghosts there tonight!"

The three pals walk towards Ottoline's house, with the pumpkin lanterns lighting their way. Suddenly, they hear a cry of "Stand and deliver!" as two masked figures jump out from behind a tree. "Freddy and Ferdy!" says Rupert. "They're dressed as highwaymen!" hisses Bill. "Trick or Treat!" says Freddy, pointing a water pistol at the chums. "Hand over your goodies or you're in for a soaking!" "It's only a pie!" protests Bill. "I was going to share it with everybody at the party!"

The Foxes take the pie then say
They'll squirt the three pals anyway . . .

"They don't know when to stop – those two!"
Says Algy. "Now I'm soaked right through!"

The soaking chums complain that their
Costumes are wrecked beyond repair . . .

"Oh, no!" says Ottoline. "Poor you!
Caught by the Foxes' ambush too . . ."

"A pie!" laughs Freddy. "We'll share *that*, won't we Ferdy?" "I'll say!" nods his brother. "Half for you and half for me!" "Give it back!" says Algy, but the Foxes only squirt their water pistols and run away. "We've got a treat and we've played a trick!" chuckles Freddy as the pair disappear. "Trust them!" splutters Algy. "I'm drenched right through!" "Me too!" says Bill. "And they've stolen the pie!" "What a pair!" says Rupert. "They're always up to some sort of silly prank!"

"The Foxes have wrecked my costume!" complains Rupert as the bedraggled chums continue on their way to Nutwood Manor. "Mine too!" says Algy. "The paint has started to run." "Never mind," says Bill. "At least we'll be able to get dry at Ottoline's house. It isn't very far now. I can see it through the trees." "Oh, no!" cries Ottoline when she answers the door. "Freddy and Ferdy have got you too! Those rascals have been squirting guests all evening. I hope you don't catch colds!"

RUPERT HEARS ABOUT THE FOXES

"The Fox brothers have had their fun
By squirting simply everyone . . ."

"But that's not all!" says Rex. "This time
The pair have turned to highway crime!"

"They robbed me too!" says Willie. "Then
Just laughed – and squirted me again!"

The doorbell rings. It's Gregory –
"Whatever can the matter be?"

Ottoline tells the chums to take off their wet costumes and dry themselves straightaway. "Rex and Reggie got a soaking from the Foxes too!" she says. "It's such a shame your costumes have all been spoilt . . ." "Hello!" says Rex. "I see that Nutwood's highwaymen have ambushed you too!" "They've gone too far this time!" complains his brother. "Playing jokes is one thing, but they stole the food we were bringing to the party!" "I know!" nods Rupert. "They took Bill's pie as well . . ."

As the chums get dry, the other party guests come to see what has happened . . . "The Foxes robbed me too!" complains Willie Mouse. "*And* they gave me a squirting. 'Trick or Treat', they said – but I think it's mean!" Just then, the doorbell rings and Gregory Guineapig appears. "I've been robbed!" he wails. "Two strangers sprang out from the bushes and squirted me with water pistols!" "There, there!" says Ottoline gently. "Come in and get dry. It was only Freddy and Ferdy."

RUPERT MAKES A PLAN

"Two highwaymen! They blocked the way
Then took my party food away . . ."

"Don't worry!" Rupert says. "We'll get
Our own back on the Foxes yet!"

"We'll need balloons! One each will do –
Then I'll explain my plan to you . . ."

Next, Rupert borrows a disguise –
"To take the Foxes by surprise!"

"They took my tin of biscuits!" sobs Gregory. "I made them specially for the party – now nobody will even see what they were like!" "Don't worry!" says Rupert. "We're going to get *everything* back and teach the Foxes a lesson!" "How?" asks Bill. We'll play a trick on them!" declares Rupert. "All this dressing up in costumes has given me a good idea. We'll have to be quick, though. Everything depends on taking Freddy and Ferdy by surprise. Gather round and I'll tell you what I need . . ."

When everyone is ready, Rupert begins to explain his plan to trick the Foxes . . . "The first thing I want is balloons!" he tells Ottoline. "That's easy!" she says. "There's a spare packet we haven't opened yet . . ." "Good!" says Rupert. "You'll all need one each." The next thing he asks for is Bingo's ghost costume. "It should be just the right size," he smiles. "Right for what?" blinks the brainy pup. "Me!" laughs Rupert. "I'll need a good disguise to play the Foxes at their own game."

The chums all file out silently –
"This way!" says Rupert. "Follow me . . ."

"Find hiding places, everyone.
*This time it's **our** turn to have fun!"*

Then Rupert waits until he sees
The Foxes, moving through the trees . . .

He puts on Bingo's costume, then
Walks back to Ottoline's again . . .

Shortly after Rupert has explained his plan, a strange procession moves silently away from Nutwood Manor . . . "We'll cut across the common!" hisses Rupert. "Quiet as you can now, everyone." The pals follow Rupert until they reach the start of the path to Ottoline's house. "This looks a good spot!" he says. "I'll get ready, while you all find places to hide. Whatever happens, don't come out until you hear me call!" "Right!" nods Bill as he and Podgy duck behind a tree . . .

No sooner has the last of his chums taken shelter, than Rupert spots two familiar-looking figures, lurking by the side of the road. "Freddy and Ferdy!" he gasps. "I *knew* they'd still be on the prowl! I'd better get ready for them straightaway." Draped in Bingo's ghostly costume, Rupert is impossible to recognise. Carrying a basket of goodies, he sets off along the path towards Nutwood Manor, as if he was arriving at the fancy-dress party for the first time.

RUPERT IS CHASED

The Foxes jump out. "Stop!" they cry
As Ottoline's new guest goes by . . .

"Shan't!" Rupert says and runs away.
The Foxes call for him to stay.

"Just wait!" calls Freddy. "Nobody
Escapes from us that easily!"

Then Rupert stops. He turns around,
Throws off the sheet and stands his ground!

As Rupert passes by, the Fox brothers jump out, waving their water pistols. "Stop!" calls Ferdy. "Trick or Treat!" cries his brother. "Hand over your basket, whoever you are . . ." "Shan't!" replies Rupert. "Ghosts aren't frightened by footpad foxes! You'll have to catch me, if you can . . ." Freddy and Ferdy are so surprised that they don't even squirt Rupert as he hurries away. "Hey! Wait!" calls Freddy. "We know you're not *really* a ghost. Come back and give us those goodies."

Rupert runs off along the path, with the Fox brothers close behind . . . "You won't get away that easily!" warns Freddy. "Halloween's the night for tricks and nobody out-tricks us . . ." Suddenly, Rupert stops and throws off his ghostly disguise. "That's where you're wrong!" he laughs. "Rupert!" blinks Ferdy. "But you've already been to Ottoline's party!" "That's right!" nods his brother. "We caught him with Bill and Algy Pug. What's going on? Why are you wearing another costume?"

RUPERT TRICKS THE FOX BROTHERS

He laughs as the dumbfounded pair
See all the Nutwood chums are there . . .

"A trap!" cries Freddy Fox. "Oh, no!
They've all brought water bombs to throw!"

"Take that!" calls Reggie. "Serves you right!
The Fox Brothers are put to flight . . .

"A pond!" wails Freddy. "Ferdy, wait!
The pair can't stop though, it's too late!

To the Foxes' astonishment, they suddenly find themselves surrounded by guests from Ottoline's party. "This time, we've tricked you!" laughs Rupert. Each pal is carrying a large balloon filled with water . . . "Help!" cries Ferdy, but it is too late. Water bombs sail towards the pair from every side, drenching them to the skin. "Take that!" cries Bill. "And this!" calls Ottoline. "There are plenty more treats for you two. Everyone *you* squirted has come to get their revenge!"

"Stop!" cries Ferdy. "It's not fair!" "Oh, yes it is!" laughs Reggie Rabbit. "You just don't like it when other people are playing tricks on *you* . . ." "Run for it!" calls Freddy, dashing off through the trees. Ferdy follows close behind, but in the darkness the pair lose their way and plunge straight into a muddy pond. "I can't stop!" gasps Freddy. "Neither can I!" wails Ferdy. One after the other, they slip on the mud and go tumbling forward, into the icy water . . .

RUPERT ENJOYS THE PARTY

"It's your turn now!" laughs Gregory.
"Just like when you both squirted me!"

"Come on!" says Rupert. "Everyone
Is even now. We've had our fun . . ."

The Foxes promise to restore
The stolen party gifts once more . . .

They dry themselves, then both join in
Just as the party treats begin . . .

"No more!" pleads Freddy as the chums all gather round. "Now you know what it's like!" says Bill. "Exactly!" nods Gregory. "It's not so much fun when you're on the receiving end, is it?" "No!" shivers Ferdy. "And we're even colder and wetter than you were!" "Come on!" laughs Rupert, hauling him to his feet. "We've *all* had enough of pranks for one night, I think. You'd better get changed and dry before you both catch dreadful colds. Come with us, back to Ottoline's party . . ."

On the way back to Nutwood Manor, Freddy and Ferdy stop to retrieve the stolen goodies. "Bravo!" smiles Rupert. "Now we'll *all* be able to have a slice of pumpkin pie . . ." Mrs Otter wraps the pair in dressing gowns and puts their clothes to dry by the fire. "I hope you've had fun!" she asks. "Yes, thanks!" laughs Rupert. "We've finished with tricks till next Halloween and there are plenty of treats here for everyone!"

SPOT THE DIFFERENCE

These two pictures look identical, but there are ten differences between them. Can you spot them all?

1. Ribbon missing from Bill's parcel; 2. Stripe missing from Bill's trousers; 3. Doorknob missing; 4. Streamer missing (above Willie Mouse); 5. Headlamp missing from Rupert's toy car; 6. Picture missing from frame; 7. Cake missing from plate; 8. Bingo's bow-tie missing; 9. Balloon missing (above Bingo); 10. Mrs Bear's brooch missing.

RUPERT and

Today's a very special day.
It's Rupert's birthday. Hip-hooray!

One day in early November, Rupert Bear wakes up with a big smile on his face. Today is his birthday! He has been counting down the days, and he can't wait to celebrate this afternoon. There will be cake and presents and games, and all his chums will be there too! After breakfast, Rupert helps his Mummy and Daddy prepare for the party. "Rupert, would you tidy up the front garden?" his mummy asks, and Rupert agrees.

the Time Machine

But first, before the gifts and cake
His Mummy sends him out to rake.

While Rupert rakes, he hears a call.
It's Jacko, waving from the wall.

It's a sunny, crisp autumn day, and Rupert is happy to be outside. There are leaves strewn all over the ground, and Rupert is just starting to rake when he hears a voice. "Hello, Rupert! And happy birthday!" It's his friend Jacko the Toy Monkey! Rupert smiles back. "I'm just going to rake this pile of leaves," he explains. "Then let me help!" Jacko offers. Working together, the pair collect the leaves in a large cart.

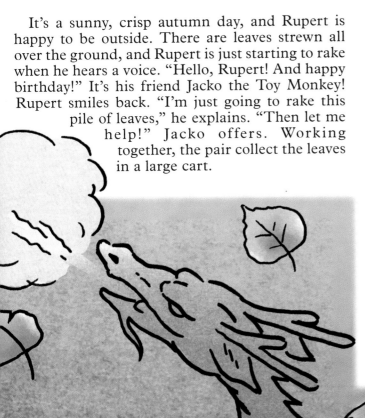

It's time to clear the leaves away.
"We'll go together," they both say.

RUPERT RAKES THE GARDEN

Beside the castle, burning bright,
A crackling bonfire is alight.

"Let's add our leaves," said Rupert Bear,
And lifts them up, into the air.

But then a gust of wind blows by,
And whisks the leaves into the sky.

The leaves whirl round, and with a puff,
They blow into the Gruffenhuff!

Jacko tells Rupert about a large bonfire in the castle grounds. "We could add these leaves to that," he says. "We have just enough time to take the leaves there, and be back for the party," Rupert says. And so the two take turns pushing the cart along the path. By the time they arrive, the bonfire is already going. It's warm and quite pleasant, and Rupert and Jacko stand for a moment, watching the flames crackling away merrily. Then Rupert grabs a handful of leaves to toss on the fire.

But at that very moment, Rupert is caught by surprise as a sudden gust of wind sweeps the leaves up and away from the bonfire! They whirl through the air, over the castle wall and into the castle gardens. Sitting in the garden is the Gruffenhuff, who's enjoying his midday meal. The Gruffenhuff drops his fork and roars out in anger. Like all ogres, he doesn't like to be disturbed while he's eating! And he especially doesn't like his meals being ruined!

RUPERT GOES TO THE CASTLE

He thunders over, with a glare,
And waves his arms at Rupert Bear.

The ogre roars, and starts to say,
"You've spoiled my meal. I'll make you pay!"

The ogre's dragon then takes flight,
And gives the chums an awful fright.

A friendly witch is there as well.
She wants to help, so casts a spell . . .

The Gruffenhuff storms out of the castle in a huff, stomping towards Rupert and Jacko! Worse, he's brought his pet dragon and three toy soldiers with him! "Oh dear," Rupert mutters nervously. "What do we do now?" Jacko whispers back. "Who threw leaves in my face?" shouts the Gruffenhuff. "Who interrupted my midday meal?" Rupert, very pale in the face, tries to explain that nobody wanted to upset the ogre, or even throw leaves. "The wind just blew them . . ." he starts to explain.

But the grumpy ogre is in no mood to listen to the little bear. He stomps again, and his pet dragon takes to the air, spitting out flames and burning the bonfire to cinders. "Now wait a moment!" calls a small but firm voice. Everyone turns around to look. It's a friendly witch, who had been passing by. "I saw the whole thing. It wasn't the little bear's fault!" she says. The Gruffenhuff is still growling, so the witch decides that the best course is to magic Rupert and Jacko safely back to their home.

RUPERT ANGERS THE OGRE

So ogre, monkey and the bear
Are magicked up into the air!

But as they land, it now appears
They've gone ahead one hundred years!

"What's this?" calls Rupert. "Can this be?
I'm talking to another me?"

"I'm going home! I've had enough!"
Declares the grumpy Gruffenhuff.

The friendly witch rubs her hands together, and chants a spell. But the wind has picked up again, and her spell catches not only Rupert and Jacko, but also the Gruffenhuff, his pet dragon and his three toy soldiers. They are all swept up into the air together. Rupert sees a swirl of colours and a flash of light. "Jacko?" he calls. "I'm still here!" his chum replies. They are turned around once more . . . and then they land in Rupert's garden with a bump! As Rupert stands up to look around, he gets a big surprise! There, standing right in front of him, is another Rupert Bear! The new Rupert blinks and says, "Rupert?" "Yes, I'm Rupert . . ." "But so am I!" They don't know what to make of it! Then Jacko shouts, "Rupert, look! Your house and garden have changed! It's like they're from another time!" "*When* are we?" Rupert asks. The new Rupert says, "It's the year 2020, of course!" The witch's spell went awry and sent them forwards one hundred years!

RUPERT TRAVELS THROUGH TIME

The chums go back to Mrs Bear,
Who cannot help but stop and stare.

She's dazed at first, but thankfully,
She makes them all a cup of tea.

The future Rupert wants to know,
Where did the grumpy ogre go?

"I have a thought. Let's take a look,"
Says Mummy Bear, "inside this book."

While both past and future Rupert marvel over this, the Gruffenhuff is gathering his dragon and toy soldiers. "I don't know what you've done, but I don't like it!" he rumbles. "I'm going home!" He storms through the gate and off towards Nutwood Common. "Come inside," says the future Rupert. "Mummy will be so surprised!" Indeed, Mrs Bear stares in wonder, and listens carefully as Rupert from the past explains what has happened. "I think we all need a cup of tea," she manages to say.

The future Rupert wants to help his new chum. "And I do wonder, where did the ogre go? He doesn't live in Nutwood now, so where was his home one hundred years ago?" Mrs Bear has an idea. She takes out her copy of A History of Nutwood. The bears pore over the pages of the book. Rupert from the future is fascinated by the old photographs from one hundred years ago. "I can't believe so many things in Nutwood look so different now," he says.

RUPERT AND RUPERT GO TO TEA

They read the Nutwood history,
And guess where Gruffenhuff might be.

So off they set, and soon it's clear,
The Gruffenhuff has just been here!

"That ogre is a frightful one!"
Moans Bill. "He's ruined all our fun!"

"And then he gave me such a scare,"
Cries Pong-Ping to the little bear.

And then they come across a passage about the Gruffenhuff. "It says here that he lived in the castle . . ." Mummy begins. "Wait a minute!" future Rupert cheers. "I recognise that castle. My old friend the Professor lives there now!" "We must go and warn your friend!" says Jacko. "Do be careful," Mrs Bear instructs. Rupert, Rupert and Jacko start off together. As they reach Nutwood Common, they spot a group of Rupert's chums. It's Bill Badger, Podgy Pig and Rastus Mouse! "What's happened here?" Rupert asks. "A grumpy ogre came crashing through," Bill sighs. "He burst our ball and spoiled our fun!" "Yes, that's the Gruffenhuff!" Rupert replies. They continue along, and there's Pong-Ping, Rupert's Pekinese friend. "An ogre just came through with a dragon," Pong-Ping cries. "The ogre was angry! He told his dragon to burn down the stile! Poor dragon. I don't think he wanted to do it." "We're going to find the Gruffenhuff," Rupert says, and Pong-Ping replies, "Then I'd better come too."

RUPERT READS AN OLD BOOK

"Us too!" adds Edward, with dismay.
"He stole our food, then stomped away!"

One Rupert leads the growing crowd.
"We must be close," he thinks aloud.

The poor Professor tries to guess,
What could have caused this dreadful mess!

"This castle was the ogre's home,"
Says Rupert, "Look! It's in this tome!"

Further ahead, the group meets Algy Pug and Edward Trunk. "Hello, what's wrong?" Rupert asks. "Hi, Rupert," Algy says glumly. "We came out to Nutwood Common for a picnic, but an ogre and his toy soldiers rushed by, and they stole all our food. The ogre was so cross, and we couldn't stop them!" Rupert introduces the Rupert from the past, and tells his chums how they're going to find the Gruffenhuff. "Good luck," Edward says, encouragingly. So on they go, and soon the Professor's castle is in sight. Rupert, Rupert, Jacko and Pong-Ping get closer, and they see the Professor and his assistant, Bodkin. They wave hello, but the Professor is frowning as he looks around, where books and pieces of furniture have been thrown out of the window. "Oh dear," the Professor sighs. "Someone has been in my house while Bodkin and I were out on a walk." "I think I can guess who it was!" Rupert says. "It must have been the Gruffenhuff!"

RUPERT TALKS TO THE PROFESSOR

The wise Professor says with pride,
"I've got a plan: first, peek inside."

He tells the bears, and Jacko too,
To find a window with a view.

So Jacko crouches, very still,
As Rupert climbs the window sill.

The ogre doesn't seem to care,
About the mess he's made in there!

First, past Rupert introduces himself and explains what has happened so far. He shows the Professor Mrs Bear's History of Nutwood. The Professor nods his head. "Well of course time travel is possible," he says, "there are many strange things in this universe!" But right now, the Professor's attention is focused on his castle. "We need to get inside, to look into this more." He suggests they peek in through the window, to work out which room the Gruffenhuff is in.

Future Rupert offers to look inside as the Professor and Bodkin begin gathering up what the ogre threw outside. Jacko crouches down and gives Rupert a boost up on his back. Meanwhile, past Rupert watches to make sure he doesn't fall. But future Rupert has steady feet as he inches towards the window sill. He sighs with relief when he sees that the Gruffenhuff is fast asleep in a chair, with his dragon snoozing under the table. But what a mess! The ogre has eaten *all* the Professor's food!

RUPERT LOOKS IN THE WINDOW

"The ogre's dreadful," Rupert cries.
"Just come this way," his friend replies.

"I've got a secret door, you see.
I know the way, so follow me!"

A trapdoor opens. Could it be,
They've made it to the library?

The old man mutters to himself,
And finds a book up on the shelf.

Rupert climbs down carefully, and the chums go back over to the Professor, tiptoeing quietly so they don't accidentally wake the ogre. The Professor listens carefully as Rupert describes what he saw and then asks Bodkin if he would wait at the front of the path and warn anyone else who might come this way. "Now come with me," he says to the four friends. "There is another, secret way into the castle . . ." The Professor pulls back a branch and reveals a large, wooden door!

"This passage will take us right to where we need to go," says the Professor. "Yes, but where is that?" Pong-Ping asks. The Professor smiles. "Just wait and see . . ." Soon, the Professor leads the friends up a ladder, through a trapdoor . . . and into his library! "My library has all the answers!" the Professor declares. He scans row after row of books, until he finds the volume he's been looking for. It's an old Rupert adventure from 1920! "That's me on the cover!" past Rupert marvels.

"Read this," he says, "and then we'll know,
What happened all those years ago!"

The chums work out a plan at last,
To send the bear back to the past.

Then Pong-Ping has a role to play:
To take the dragon far away.

The dragon's playful in the end,
He really wants to be their friend!

"Yes, but something is wrong," frowns the Professor, as he riffles through the pages. "Here you are at the beginning, but then you and Jacko . . . and the Gruffenhuff too . . . have disappeared from the remaining pages." "What does that mean?" Rupert asks. "We have to get you all back to your own time," the Professor says. "But since magic brought you here, you'll need magic to take you back. I suggest you go to the Wise Old Goat. He'll be able to help." "But what if the Gruffenhuff wakes up first?" Rupert asks. "He might tell his dragon to burn your castle down!" "I know all about dragons," Pong-Ping speaks up. "The Gruffenhuff's dragon looks just like my dragon, Ming. I think he only burns things when the ogre makes him. Maybe he'll come with me instead." So the friends tiptoe towards the kitchen. Pong-Ping quietly opens the door and speaks soothingly to the dragon. As he guessed, the dragon just wants to be friends, and happily follows Pong-Ping out.

RUPERT HATCHES A PLAN

They leave before the ogre wakes,
And hope there will be no mistakes!

The Wise Old Goat breathes in and stares.
"What's this? I see two Rupert Bears?"

The chums explain. And then they say,
"It's been a most exciting day!"

"There's something that I have in mind,"
The Goat says. "Let's see what we find!"

Still mindful of the sleeping ogre, the chums wave goodbye to the Professor and hurridly make their way down the hill, back towards Nutwood Common. Pong-Ping says that he'll look after the dragon while the others visit the Wise Old Goat, but he promises to join them at Rupert's party later. "This way," future Rupert says, and past Rupert and Jacko follow. The Wise Old Goat lives in another castle, not far away. He sits up at once when he sees two Rupert Bears approaching.

"What's this?" he says. "Two Ruperts? Am I seeing double?" "Oh, no, it's me," says future Rupert, "and it's also me, but from one hundred years ago! You see, it's been the most exciting day . . ." And the three friends tell the Old Goat what's happened so far, and explain why they need his help. "We need some sort of magic to send me back home," says past Rupert. "Let me see," the Wise Old Goat replies. "I'm sure there's something here that will do the trick . . ."

RUPERT VISITS THE WISE OLD GOAT

"This camera might just do the trick.
But hurry up – we must be quick!"

They run as swiftly as they can,
To finally complete their plan.

His Mummy says, "I'll bake more, too,
For all your guests, both old and new."

The chums work hard. They must invite
All of their friends, to get it right.

"Ah-ha!" the Wise Old Goat cries. "Here is a time camera. All we have to do is set the date. Then when we take a photograph, everyone in the picture will be sent back to the right time." "Hurry, let's take it now!" says Jacko, but the Old Goat shakes his head. "We can only take the photo if the whole group from 1920 is together," he explains. Future Rupert has an idea. "Let's go home and invite everyone to my party. We'll take the photo there!" The chums race home quick as they can.

Rupert runs inside, where Mrs Bear is baking cakes and treats for his birthday. When Rupert explains their plan, Mrs Bear agrees to make more cakes and cookies for all the guests, both old and new. "I'll help make invites," Jacko offers. "But how can we get the Gruffenhuff to come too?" future Rupert wonders. "He might still be mad!" "Why don't you bring him some cakes?" Mummy suggests. "Yes, he'll come along for sure if there's food!" past Rupert agrees.

To lure the grumpy ogre there,
They take some cakes from Mrs Bear.

By now, the Gruffenhuff's awake,
And very tempted by the cake.

While everybody mills about,
Wise Goat takes the time camera out.

"Oh, may we take a photo, please?"
Says Rupert. "Ready? Now, say 'cheese'!"

Jacko leaves to hand out invites to everyone, while the two Ruperts head back to the castle. The bears laugh and joke along the way. They're already the best of friends! When they reach the castle, they see the Gruffenhuff right away. By now, he's awake, and not quite as grumpy as before. And he cheers up even more when Rupert hands him an invitation and some of Mrs Bear's cakes. "There will be more cake at my party . . ." he promises, and the ogre agrees to come.

Later that day, Rupert's chums arrive one by one for his party. "Happy birthday, Rupert!" they cheer, and say hello to past Rupert as well. Pong-Ping brings the dragon, and then the Gruffenhuff arrives, with his toy soldiers close behind. Now that everyone is here, the Wise Old Goat takes the camera out and sets the dial to 1920. Then he winks at Rupert Bear. "Oh, let's take a photo of all our special guests!" Rupert announces. "And then we'll have cake . . ."

RUPERT RETURNS TO THE CASTLE

The camera flashes with a blast,
And sends the chums back to the past!

The magic's worked (though who knows how?).
The year is 1920 now!

Because the Wise Goat set the date,
They're home in time to celebrate!

"A happy birthday!" Rupert cheers,
"To Rupert Bear, all through the years!"

Everyone agrees, even the ogre, and they line up in front of the camera. The Rupert from the future has just enough time to wave at Rupert from the past, and then everyone says, "Cheese!" *Flash!* The camera goes off, and Rupert sees a sparkling light. Once again, Rupert, Jacko, the Gruffenhuff, the dragon and the toy soldiers are whisked up into the air. They twist and tumble around . . . and find themselves back in 1920, right in Rupert's garden, where his birthday party has just started. "So the Wise Old Goat set the right date!" Jacko smiles. "Look, there's Rupert!" his friends call out in surprise. "You weren't here a moment ago, but you're here now. Where did you come from?" "Never mind that," Rupert laughs. "Now it's time to celebrate." "Happy Birthday, Rupert!" everyone cheers, as they watch Mrs Bear light the birthday candles. Rupert smiles and secretly wishes his friend from 2020 a happy birthday as well!

THE END

SPOT THE DIFFERENCE

Rupert, Rupert and Jacko are visiting the Wise Old Goat.
There are 9 differences between the two pictures. Can you spot them all?

93

RUPERT and

*Here's Rika, Rupert's Lapp friend, who
Is staying for a day or two.*

When Santa's reindeer aren't pulling his sleigh at Christmas, they live in Lapland, where they are looked after by a little girl called Rika. Rupert and Rika are good friends and have agreed that she will stop off on her journey home to spend a day or two in Nutwood. Rupert's parents are delighted to see her when she arrives late one evening, having left her reindeer tied up in Pong-Ping's garden, where there's plenty of room.

the Stolen Snowman

The reindeer herd she had to bring
Are being cared for by Pong-Ping.

"Tomorrow," Rupert says, "we should
Be able to explore Nutwood."

Later that evening, when Rupert and Rika take a last look out of the window before going to their rooms, the night is clear and moonlight glistens on the snow. "Doesn't it look lovely," smiles Rupert. "Yes," agrees Rika, "so calm and still." Long after the pair have said goodnight and gone to bed, Rupert is woken by the howling of the wind. Instead of calm moonlight outside, he sees thick snow flashing past his bedroom window . . .

But in the night it starts to snow
And howling winds begin to blow . . .

RUPERT SPOTS BILLY BLIZZARD

Rupert peers out, then rubs his eyes
As past his room, a snowman flies!

Then Rupert sees someone he knows
Who seems to guide the raging snows . . .

"It's Billy Blizzard!" Rupert cries
As off the frosty figure flies.

"Whatever's wrong?" asks Mrs Bear.
"It's Billy Blizzard! He's out there!"

Rupert jumps out of bed and opens the window. It is almost snatched from his grasp by the swirling white storm which rages outside. He peers out and gives a cry of amazement as he sees his snowman, which has been standing in the garden, caught up by the storm and carried away on the wind. As the snowman spins past his window, the storm seems to clear and Rupert sees a familiar-looking figure standing outside, directing the snow with a jagged icicle.

"It's Billy Blizzard!" Rupert's cry rings out above the noise of the wind, and the sinister figure turns to give him a wicked grin. The next minute he leaps up after the tail of the snowstorm and is carried away into the night. "Rupert! Whatever's the matter? Do shut that window!" says Mrs Bear, who has heard Rupert call out. Rika has heard him too and comes to see what's happening. "It was Billy Blizzard!" Rupert cries. "I saw him out there, standing in the garden."

RUPERT AND RIKA SEE JACK FROST

"He's Jack Frost's cousin who was sent
To the South Pole as punishment."

"He's gone and there's no damage done
So back to bed now everyone . . ."

Next morning Rupert's keen to show
Rika the sights, so off they go.

"Look!" Rupert cries, amazed as they
See Jack Frost almost straightaway . . .

"Who's Billy Blizzard?" asks Rika. Rupert explains that he's Jack Frost's cousin, who was banished to the Frozen South by Jack's father, King Frost, because he kept making terrifying blizzards. "Ever since then, he's been a sworn enemy of the King. That was one of his blizzards just now. It was so strong that it carried off my snowman!" "Well, there's nothing we can do about it now," says Mrs Bear. "Back to bed, everybody. Try to get a good night's sleep."

Next morning Rupert and Rika agree not to spoil the first day of her visit by worrying about Billy Blizzard. As soon as they have finished breakfast, they set off to have a proper look round Nutwood. No one is about as they head across the common to the top of a hill from where, Rupert tells Rika, you can see the whole of the village. They are almost there when Rupert spots somebody scanning the horizon with a telescope. "Look!" he cries. "It's Jack Frost."

RUPERT HEARS ABOUT THE SNOWMEN

He turns around and greets the pair
Then tells them what he's doing there.

"I've come to look for snowmen, though
It seems that Nutwood's none to show!"

"That's Billy Blizzard's work, I'm sure!"
Gasps Rupert and tells what he saw . . .

"Each year Jack takes them to the King –
Now Blizzard's ruined everything!"

Jack is so intent on studying Nutwood through his telescope that he doesn't notice Rika and Rupert until they reach the top of the hill. "Why, Rupert!" he exclaims. "I was just about to try and find you. But who's this?" Rupert introduces Rika, who says she's delighted to meet Jack Frost at last. "What did you want me for?" Rupert asks. "I hoped you'd be able to tell me what's happened to all the snowmen around here," says Jack. "There's not a single one to be seen!"

"I can tell you what happened to *my* snowman!" Rupert cries. As he hears about last night's blizzard, Jack Frost looks more and more grim. "It's plain that Billy has taken them all to get back at my father," he declares. Rika looks bewildered, so Rupert explains that each year, just before the thaw, Jack comes to collect all the snowmen and take them to his father's palace. "Now I've got to find a way to get this year's snowmen back from Billy Blizzard!" says Jack.

RUPERT'S PAL RIKA HAS A PLAN

"I'll have to try and get them back
From Billy's fortress!" declares Jack.

They'll all go there, the three decide
On Santa's reindeer, which they'll ride.

It's all arranged, but even so
Rupert must ask if he may go.

"Of course you may," says Mrs Bear.
"But keep warm if it's chilly there."

Jack explains that he's sure Billy Blizzard has taken the missing snowmen to his ice fortress in the Frozen South. "The trouble is, I can't call up a wind to fly there as it's the wrong part of the world . . ." "I'm sure Santa wouldn't mind you borrowing his reindeer," Rika suggests. "You mean you'd really lend them to me?" cries Jack. "Of course, I'd have to come too," says Rika, "to make sure they're all right." "Then so must I," declares Rupert, stoutly.

Although he's keen to join the others, Rupert knows that he has to ask his mother first. "I'll come with you," says Jack as Rika hurries off to Pong-Ping's house to get the reindeer ready. Mrs Bear has met Jack Frost before and knows that Rupert has always returned safely from their adventures together. When she hears what's happened, and that Rika will be going too, she agrees to let Rupert go and help Jack but tells him to wrap up well.

RUPERT SETS OFF WITH HIS CHUMS

Then Jack and Rupert run to reach
Pong-Ping's to choose a reindeer each . . .

"I've got two saddled up for you,"
Says Rika, who checks her lasso.

The pals are ready to depart:
At Rika's word their flight will start . . .

"Hold tight now!" Rika warns as they
Take off, then calls, "Up and away!"

Rupert and Jack hurry to Pong-Ping's house where Rika has prepared three of her reindeer for the long flight to the Frozen South. Her face lights up when she hears that Rupert can come too. Pong-Ping has agreed to look after the other reindeer and is introducing himself to Jack Frost when Rupert notices that Rika is tying a coil of rope to her saddle. "What's that?" he asks her. "A reindeer herdsman's lasso," Rika replies. "I always carry it with me on a long journey."

Daylight is fading by the time Rupert and the others are ready to set off. The reindeer usually fly only at night because Santa prefers them not to be seen. But since Pong-Ping's house is well away from the village and as it's nearly dark already, Rika agrees that this time they may start straightaway. "Good luck!" cries Pong-Ping as the three chums mount up. "Up and away!" calls Rika and in no time at all the three reindeer are soaring up into the darkening sky.

RUPERT SEES A STRANGE STAR

Jack leads the way through starry skies
To where his cousin's fortress lies.

"Look!" Rika cries as a strange light
Flies towards them through the dark night . . .

"A shooting star?" asks Jack. But no,
It can't be for it's far too slow.

Then Rupert gasps aloud and blinks:
Can the strange light be what he thinks?

Night falls and soon Rupert has the feeling he is flying among the stars. Although Rika is in charge of the reindeer it is Jack Frost who decides upon their course. "How can you be so sure you're right?" Rupert asks him. "When my father banished Billy Blizzard he exiled him to the Frozen South," says Jack. "I know where . . ." Before he can finish Rika breaks in with a cry of, "Look! There's a strange light ahead of us. What can it be? It seems to be coming this way!"

"Perhaps it's a shooting star?" suggests Jack. "Then it's like none I've ever seen," answers Rika as the light weaves its way towards them. "Too slow and wobbly." To Rupert's surprise the light seems oddly familiar and as it gets closer a thought grows in his mind. "It couldn't be, surely," he whispers. "What did you say?" asks Rika. But Rupert is too excited to answer. For now he is sure he knows what the strange light is. "How extraordinary!" he gasps. "It *is* him!"

RUPERT MEETS THE SAGE OF UM

"The Sage of Um!" laughs Rupert, "Why,
It's his lamp *we saw in the sky!"*

How does a Nutwood snowman come
To be there with the Sage of Um?

"A blizzard blew past suddenly
And dropped him here, right next to me!"

The snowman asks if they can go
To Nutwood but the Sage says no.

"The Sage of Um!" cries Rupert. His friends see that the light is really a lantern hanging from the handle of a large, upturned umbrella in which sits an old man dressed in a long gown. "An unexpected pleasure!" smiles the Sage as Rupert introduces him to Rika and Jack, explaining that the Sage is an old friend. "It's been a night of strange meetings," laughs the Sage and gestures to the snowman who's sitting alongside him. "You'll never guess how I met him!"

It turns out that the Sage was flying towards his home on the island of Um when a blizzard suddenly appeared from nowhere. "I dived down to get out of the way," he explains, "but scraped the underneath of the storm cloud. That's when this snowman appeared. Must have fallen out of the cloud. What am I to do with him?" "Take me back to Nutwood," pipes up the Snowman. "I'm afraid I can't," says the Sage. "I have to get back to Um island without delay."

RUPERT IS JOINED BY A SNOWMAN

The Sage must fly to Um, so Jack
Says they will take the snowman back.

The snowman manages to climb
On Rupert's reindeer in no time.

Then, waving everyone goodbye,
The Sage soars off across the sky.

The snowman learns where they are bound
And begs Rupert to turn around.

"What's the matter?" asks Rupert. "It's the unicorns!" replies the Sage, who looks after the only unicorn herd in the whole world. "They've all caught bad colds, I'm afraid. I've got to get back and make sure that they're all right." "In that case we'll take the snowman," says Jack. "He ought to be with me, anyway." "He can ride on my reindeer," says Rupert and flies closer to the Brella. The snowman smiles and eagerly clambers up behind Rupert.

"Nice to meet you!" calls the Sage as he whisks away. "We must hurry," says Jack. "Forward!" cries Rika and off bound the reindeer. "No! Wait!" squeaks the snowman. "There must be a mistake! This is the way Billy Blizzard went!" "Of course!" says Rupert. "We're going after him to make him give back the snowmen he stole from Nutwood . . ." "But I've just got away from him," whimpers the snowman. "He might catch me again. Oh, no don't go on, please!"

RUPERT ARRIVES AT BILLY'S FORT

"We can't," says Jack, "until we free
The other snowmen, don't you see!"

Just then the sky begins to glow,
For Blizzard's fortress lies below.

Around the fort the three friends see
A snowstorm rages constantly . . .

"He'll see us if we fly too near,"
Says Jack. "Let's land and walk from here."

"How selfish!" thinks Rupert. "I'm glad he isn't mine." "Please turn back, Jack Frost!" begs the snowman. "I don't want to be one of Billy Blizzard's slaves." "Nor do the other snowmen he stole!" snaps Jack. "Can't *you* get him to turn back?" the snowman appeals to Rupert and Rika. But neither replies for, in the growing light, they can see something ahead. "Can that be . . . ?" Rika begins. "Yes," Jack says quietly. "It's Billy Blizzard's stronghold."

The reindeer slow to a halt. The whimpering of the snowman is the only sound as Rupert and the others gaze at the grim ice fortress, which is surrounded by a moat bristling with spears of ice. The only entrance is over a drawbridge, which is firmly closed. There is no chance of flying in on the reindeer, for a constant blizzard swirls fiercely above the walls. "We must land somewhere out of sight and decide what to do," says Jack. The snowman gives a low moan.

Rupert and the Stolen Snowmen
RUPERT HAS AN IDEA

*They circle low, until they find
Some ice slabs they can hide behind.*

*"Come on!" calls Jack and scrambles to
The top to get a better view.*

*How can they get inside the fort
To free the snowmen who've been caught?*

*Then Rupert has a good idea,
"We'll get Blizzard to come out here!"*

"We'd be out of sight down there," says Rupert, pointing to a flat stretch of snow behind some ice slabs which face Billy Blizzard's fortress. The snowman groans. Jack, though, agrees with Rupert, so Rika leads the way down in a wide sweep and lands behind the ridge of ice. The three friends dismount at once and scramble up to the top in order to spy out the land. The snowman stays put, dismally gazing after them and snivelling quietly to himself.

When they reach the top of the ridge, Rupert, Rika and Jack gaze glumly at the sight that greets them. Between the ice slabs and the fortress is a stretch of open ground, then a moat, filled with ice spears. Above the walls a blizzard rages wildly. "I just can't see a way of getting in," Jack sighs. "Nor can I," declares Rika. "We may not have to get *in* at all," says Rupert. "All we need to do to free the snowmen is make Billy Blizzard come *out*."

105

RUPERT PLEADS WITH THE SNOWMAN

"But how?" asks Jack. Rupert replies,
"We'll lure him with a tempting prize!"

"A snowman!" cries Jack. "Yes, I see!
But do you think ours will agree?"

"Oh, no!" the snowman wails, "You can't
Use me as bait. You won't, I shan't!"

"Please!" Rupert says, "It's up to you
To help us free the others too!"

"How?" asks Jack. "We have to tempt him," says Rupert and points to the dismal snowman waiting below. "I'm sure Billy Blizzard won't be able to resist a chance to recapture the prisoner he lost on the way from Nutwood!" "But that cowardly snowman will never agree to act as bait!" says Rika. "We must try!" says Jack. "Our only hope is to lure Billy out, then grab him and make him hand over all the snowmen." "Come on," he calls. "Let's make a start!"

The snowman is aghast when he hears Rupert's plan. "You must be potty!" he gasps. "I only just escaped being one of his slaves!" Seeing that the others are about to lose their tempers with the timid snowman, Rupert makes a last appeal for help. "I know it's asking an awful lot," he says, "but it's the only way your fellow snowmen can be saved from a miserable life of slavery under a cruel and wicked master." The snowman gulps but says nothing.

The snowman thinks, then gives a sigh –
"You're right!" he says. "I have to try!"

As soon as Blizzard comes in sight
Rika's lasso will bind him tight.

The others watch the snowman who
Gets ready to step into view.

He nears the fort and then they see
The drawbridge crash down suddenly . . .

The snowman stares at his feet for a long time. Then he looks up at Rupert. "All right!" he says. "But I'm still scared." "Heroes often are," says Jack. "Me?" the snowman scoffs. "Not a heroic snowflake in my body." So it's agreed: the snowman will show himself on the open stretch of snow in front of the fortress. "Wait a moment," Rupert says. "What if Billy Blizzard runs inside again as soon as he sees us?" "Just let him try!" says Rika and reaches for her reindeer lasso.

Rupert and the others get into position and watch anxiously as the snowman slowly edges his way down to the open stretch of snow, keeping to the shadows as long as he can. He has been told to go just far enough into the open for Billy Blizzard to be able to see him. He pauses in the shadows at the foot of the slabs. Has he lost his nerve? No. He steps into the open and waits. For a long time nothing happens. Then, with a loud crash, the drawbridge slams down over the moat . . .

Next minute there's an angry shout
As Billy Blizzard charges out!

Rika lassos him expertly
But slips as Blizzard tries to flee.

The timid snowman saves the day
And stops him as he gets away!

As soon as Blizzard's safely tied
Up tight, Jack says, "Let's go inside!"

Over the drawbridge charges a furious Billy Blizzard. He brandishes an icicle dart but the snowman stands his ground. Rupert and the others, who have been crouching out of sight, jump up into view. Billy casts them a wild glance but, before he can do anything, Rika swings her lasso round in the air and drops it over his shoulders. He squeals and starts to run back to the drawbridge, jerking Rika off her feet and dragging her along with him.

Rupert and Jack scramble after Rika to try and rescue her. They needn't worry though, for the snowman launches himself at Billy, bowling him over and sending his icicle dart flying. Rika picks herself up and the others join her. In no time at all Billy Blizzard has been soundly trussed up. Jack hauls him to his feet and points towards the stronghold. "We're all going inside now," he snaps. "And you're coming with us, whether you like it or not!"

RUPERT SEES THE SNOWMEN FREED

Inside the fort Jack takes a key
And goes to set the snowmen free.

Then Rupert hears a mighty cheer
As all the prisoners appear.

"You may have set them free, but how,"
Sneers Blizzard, "will you get home now?"

"Don't worry!" Rika smiles, "We'll cope.
Tied scarves will make a splendid rope!"

Billy Blizzard snarls with rage but lets himself be led into the fortress. "Where are the snowmen?" demands Jack, taking a set of keys from the pouch on Billy's belt. Billy nods towards a nearby door. Jack unlocks it and goes through, together with the snowman. It's hard to see how Billy could look any angrier, but he scowls even more as a great cheer comes from the other room. Out march a gaggle of snowmen, with Jack and the brave snowman perched on their shoulders.

Although he's been outsmarted, Billy Blizzard isn't finished yet. As the cheering dies down he turns to Jack and sneers, "Very clever. But how will you get the snowmen to your father's palace? You can't just summon a wind like you would in the top half of the world!" "Don't worry, Jack!" cries Rika. "We'll go back to Nutwood the way we came . . ." The pals look puzzled, but Rika has a plan. "Collect the snowmen's scarves and knot them into three ropes," she calls.

RUPERT'S PAL RIKA SAVES THE DAY

*She brings the reindeer near and then
Calls, "Now all come outside again!"*

*"I understand!" cries Rupert, "You
Plan to tow all the snowmen too!"*

*The snowmen stand where they are told
So each one has a "rope" to hold . . .*

*Jack leaves a dart deliberately
For Blizzard to cut himself free.*

Mystified by Rika's request, Rupert and Jack hurry to do as she asks while she brings the reindeer round to the flat area in front of the fort. Then, as everyone looks on, she ties a scarf "rope" to each of the reindeer's saddles. "Now I understand!" cries Rupert. "We're going to tow the snowmen all the way back to Nutwood!" "That's right," laughs Rika. "The reindeer will do it easily. A few snowmen weigh next to nothing, compared with Santa's loaded sleigh."

At last all is ready for the journey back to Nutwood, where Jack will be able to summon a wind to carry him and the snowmen on to King Frost's palace. The snowmen are split into three groups and each given a "rope" to hold. Before climbing onto his reindeer, Jack takes Billy Blizzard's icicle dart and sticks it upright in the snow. "You can cut yourself free as soon as we've gone," he tells him. "Don't try to follow us or you'll have my father's ice guards to deal with!"

RUPERT FLIES BACK TO NUTWOOD

Then Rika gives a rousing cry
And all the reindeer start to fly . . .

"We'll fly to Nutwood first," says Jack,
"And then I'll take the snowmen back."

"We're almost there now!" Rupert cries.
And points down to where Nutwood lies.

The reindeer slowly circle round,
Then gently settle on the ground.

"Ready?" asks Rika. Rupert and Jack nod and she gives a shrill cry. The reindeer start trotting across the flat snow, gradually gathering speed until they bound into the air, towing the snowmen behind them. "Nutwood next stop!" laughs Rupert as they race through the sky. "The snowmen and I will go straight on as soon as we arrive in Nutwood," says Jack. "I'm afraid I'll have to go home soon too," adds Rika. "I've got to get the reindeer back to Lapland."

The light begins to grow and after a while Rupert starts to recognise the landscape down below. "Nutwood!" he cries and points excitedly to the village. "Make sure you land on the high common," says Jack. "We don't want anyone to see." Rika nods and down they start to go. The reindeer land so gently that all the snowmen are able to keep their feet as they slowly touch down. "We made it!" shouts Rupert happily. Everyone grins with delight, even the snowmen.

RUPERT BIDS RIKA FAREWELL

It's time for Jack to go now so
He gives his wind whistle a blow.

A wind starts as he waves goodbye
And whisks the snowmen through the sky.

Soon Rika must be on her way,
"I'll come back next year, if I may . . ."

"Yes!" Pong-Ping cries. "And then you'll see
The rest of Nutwood properly!"

Jack wastes no time in gathering the snowmen around him. Then he turns to Rika and Rupert and thanks them for all their help. "Thanks from my father too!" he calls as he bids them a final farewell. "I know he will be grateful for everything you've done." Taking a tiny whistle from the pouch on his belt, he gives the snowmen a sign to get ready. As soon as he blows the whistle a great wind starts to blow and whisks all the snowmen up into the air and out of sight.

That evening, as soon as it is dark, it is Rika's turn to say goodbye. She has already thanked Rupert's parents and is back in Pong-Ping's garden, ready to leave. "You really must come for a longer visit next time," Pong-Ping urges her. "I promise I shall," Rika laughs and mounts her reindeer. "Up and away!" she cries and blows a kiss to the two pals as the whole herd takes off into the night sky. "She *is* nice!" sigh Pong-Ping and Rupert together. THE END

How carefully can you colour these two pictures?

HOW TO WEAVE RUPERT'S

Do you like making things by paper folding? Here's something interesting that uses paperweaving as well as folding. To make one you will need two pieces of paper (one of them coloured, if you can manage it), and you must prepare them carefully. The length of each one should be at least three times its breadth, seven inches by two is a good size.

Fold one in half to find the middle line XX in figure 2, then carefully measure and draw one more line marked A on each side so that AX each way is exactly as long as XX.

Now the three most important lines must be drawn across the paper from A to A, one exactly in the middle and the others just half way between that line and the outside edges. These must be as exact as you can make them.

Fold the paper in half (fig. 3) and make careful scissor-cuts along your lines from the X fold to the A line and a tiny bit beyond. If you have done this neatly you should have four doubled strips all the same width. Treat the second piece of paper in exactly the same way (fig. 4). Now for the weaving. Arrange both pieces as in

114

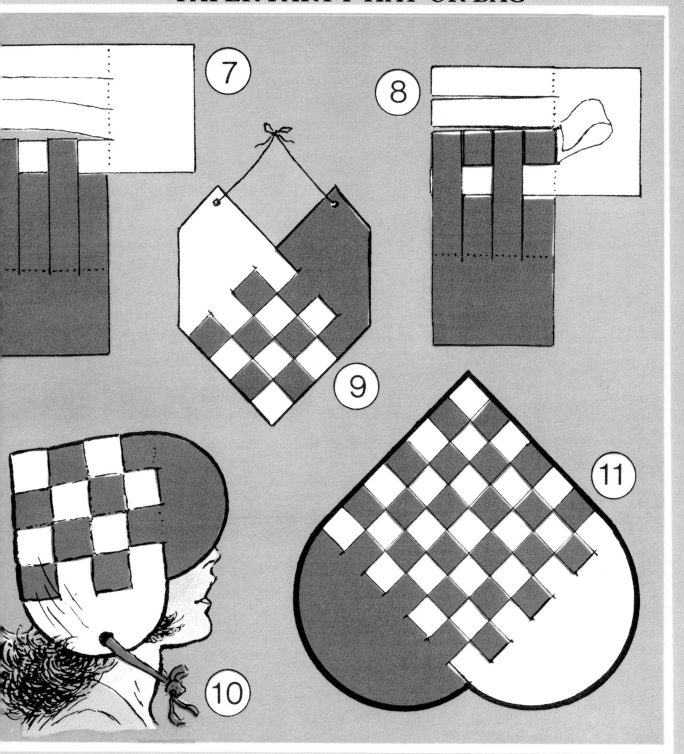

figure 5 and let the first red strip go inside the lowest white one, then push that white strip through the next red one, open it to receive the third red one and push it through the fourth. This is shown larger in figure 6. Never let a doubled strip just pass over another one. Always make one pass *through* the other.

When the lowest white strip has finished it should look like figure 7, and it can be eased down along the red strips as in figure 8 which shows that the next white strip must be bent back in a curve before it can be slipped through

the first red strip – and so on. More and more care is needed to avoid tearing the paper.

When all the strips are "woven", cut the big square ends to some nicer shape. If you cut it as in figure 9, coloured strings from near the points turn it into a little bag. If you use much bigger paper and cut curves as in figure 1, it could make a special hat for your next party (fig. 10).

If you have enjoyed this, try drawing more lines at figure 2 to make more strips. Figure 11 shows the effect if you make six cuts, giving seven equal strips to be woven.

RUPERT'S MEMORY GAME

After you have read all the stories in this book, you can play Rupert's fun Memory Game! Study the pictures below. Each is part of a bigger picture you will have seen in the stories. Can you answer the questions at the bottom of the page? Afterwards, check the stories to discover if you were right.

NOW TRY TO REMEMBER . . .

1. Why is Farmer Brown angry?
2. Who is Rupert looking for?
3. Who has dressed up as a ghost?
4. Where is Pippin going?
5. What is the dwarf carrying?
6. Why is Rupert in the water?
7. Where is the Professor going?
8. Where is Rupert being taken?

9. Why is Billy Blizzard tied up?
10. Why is Gregory upset?
11. Where is Rupert going?
12. Where is Jacko running?
13. Why are Freddy and Ferdy running away?
14. Who is Rupert's friend?
15. Where are the chums going?
16. What is Billy Blizzard doing?

FOLLOW
RUPERT
EVERY
MORNING
IN THE
**DAILY
EXPRESS**

Printed by Greycaines, Watford and London.